"Annihilation Domain!"

As Maple spoke, black wings unfurled behind her. A halo appeared, glowing dark crimson. Both the visuals and the skill name suggested none who entered would leave unharmed.

In the training room

Skills

Outclass / Attack Stance / Martial Arts X / Divine Fist X
Fisticuff Mastery X / Fisticuff Secrets VI
Magic Mastery X / HP Boost (L)
MP Boost (L) / Strength Boost (L)
Attack Boost (L) / Power Boost / Spell Boost
Poison Nullification / Paralyze Nullification / Stun Nullification
Sleep Resist (L) / Freeze Resist (M)
Burn Resist (L) / Throw / Hard Body / Iron Knuckle

Bofuri

I Don't Want to Get Hurt, so I'll Max Out My Defense.

⑫

YUUMIKAN

Illustration by KOIN

YEN ON
NEW YORK

VELVET'S STATS

Velvet

Lv 92   HP 800/800   MP 170/170
[STR 50] [VIT 30]   [AGI 60]
[DEX 10] [INT 20]

Welcome to NewWorld Online.

Bofuri

YUUMIKAN

Translation by Andrew Cunningham • Cover art by Koin

This book is a work of fiction. Names, characters, places, and incidents are the product of the author's imagination or are used fictitiously. Any resemblance to actual events, locales, or persons, living or dead, is coincidental.

ITAINO WA IYA NANODE BOGYORYOKU NI KYOKUFURI SHITAITO OMOIMASU. Vol. 12
©Yuumikan, Koin 2021
First published in Japan in 2021 by KADOKAWA CORPORATION, Tokyo.
English translation rights arranged with KADOKAWA CORPORATION, Tokyo, through TUTTLE-MORI AGENCY, INC., Tokyo.

English translation © 2024 by Yen Press, LLC

Yen Press, LLC supports the right to free expression and the value of copyright. The purpose of copyright is to encourage writers and artists to produce the creative works that enrich our culture.

The scanning, uploading, and distribution of this book without permission is a theft of the author's intellectual property. If you would like permission to use material from the book (other than for review purposes), please contact the publisher. Thank you for your support of the author's rights.

Yen On
150 West 30th Street, 19th Floor
New York, NY 10001

Visit us at yenpress.com • facebook.com/yenpress • twitter.com/yenpress
yenpress.tumblr.com • instagram.com/yenpress

First Yen On Edition: April 2024
Edited by Yen On Editorial: Leilah Labossiere, Ivan Liang
Designed by Yen Press Design: Liz Parlett

Yen On is an imprint of Yen Press, LLC.
The Yen On name and logo are trademarks of Yen Press, LLC.

The publisher is not responsible for websites (or their content) that are not owned by the publisher.

Library of Congress Cataloging-in-Publication Data
Names: Yuumikan, author. | Koin, illustrator. | Cunningham, Andrew, 1979– translator.
Title: Bofuri, I don't want to get hurt, so I'll max out my defense / Yuumikan ; illustration by Koin ; translated by Andrew Cunningham.
Other titles: Itai no wa iya nano de bōgyoryoku ni kyokufuri shitai to omoimasu. English
Description: First Yen On edition. | New York : Yen On, 2021–
Identifiers: LCCN 2020055872 | ISBN 9781975322731 (v. 1 ; trade paperback) |
ISBN 9781975323547 (v. 2 ; trade paperback) | ISBN 9781975323561 (v. 3 ; trade paperback) |
ISBN 9781975323585 (v. 4 ; trade paperback) | ISBN 9781975323608 (v. 5 ; trade paperback) |
ISBN 9781975323622 (v. 6 ; trade paperback) | ISBN 9781975323646 (v. 7 ; trade paperback) |
ISBN 9781975323660 (v. 8 ; trade paperback) | ISBN 9781975323684 (v. 9 ; trade paperback) |
ISBN 9781975367688 (v. 10 ; trade paperback) | ISBN 9781975367701 (v. 11 ; trade paperback) |
ISBN 9781975367725 (v. 12 ; trade paperback)
Subjects: LCSH: Video gamers—Fiction. | Virtual reality—Fiction. | GSAFD: Science fiction.
Classification: LCC PL874.I46 I8313 2021 | DDC 895.63/6—dc23
LC record available at https://lccn.loc.gov/2020055872

ISBNs: 978-1-9753-6772-5 (paperback)
978-1-9753-6773-2 (ebook)

10 9 8 7 6 5 4 3 2 1

LSC-C

Printed in the United States of America

CONTENTS

**I Don't Want to Get Hurt,
so I'll Max Out My Defense.**

Prologue		001
Chapter 1	Defense Build and the Diving Suits	003
Chapter 2	Defense Build and New Power	025
Chapter 3	Defense Build and the Submerged Shrine	047
Chapter 4	Defense Build and the Sunken Ship	089
Chapter 5	Defense Build and Lost Legacy	119
Chapter 6	Defense Build and the Next Event	159
Chapter 7	Defense Build and the Ninth Stratum	169
Bonus Story	Defense Build and Deep Thoughts	185
Afterword		193

NewWorld Online Status

GUILD Maple Tree

NAME Maple
LV 68
HP 200/200 **MP** 22/22

PROFILE
The Tankiest Great Shielder

She was a gaming noob, but by putting all her points in defense, she grew so tanky that all attacks just bounce right off. The kind of girl who finds fun in everything, her imaginative leaps astound those around her. When she fights, she negates all incoming attacks while unleashing a barrage of counter-skills.

STATUS
STR 000 **VIT** 18690 **AGI** 000
DEX 000 **INT** 000

EQUIPMENT
- New Moon: Hydra
- Bonding Bridge
- Night's Facsimile: Devour/Lure of the Deep
- Black Rose Armor: Saturating Chaos
- Toughness Ring
- Life Ring

SKILLS
Shield Attack Sidestep Deflect Meditation Taunt Inspire HP Boost (S) MP Boost (S) Heavy Body
Green's Grace Great Shield Mastery IX Cover Move V Cover Pierce Guard Counter Quick Change
Absolute Defense Moral Turpitude Sheep Eater Hydra Eater Bomb Eater Indomitable Guardian
Giant Killing Psychokinesis Fortress Martyr's Devotion Machine God Bug Urn Curse Zone Freeze
Pandemonium I Heaven's Throne Nether Nexus Crystallization Cataclysmic Eruption Unbreakable Shield
Twisted Resurrection Earth Wielding II Apex of Authority

TAMED MONSTER
Name Syrup A turtle with high defense
Giganticize Spirit Cannon Mother Nature etc.

NewWorld Online Status

GUILD Maple Tree

NAME Sally **LV** 70

HP 32/32 MP 130/130

PROFILE
The Unhittable Assassin

Maple's friend and partner, she's got a good head on her shoulders. Her top priority is to ensure she and Maple enjoy the game together. Light armor and twin daggers are the core of her combat style; her raw gaming talent and astonishing focus allow her to evade all attacks.

STATUS
- STR 140
- VIT 000
- AGI 185
- DEX 045
- INT 060

EQUIPMENT
- Deep Sea Dagger
- Seabed Dagger
- Surface Scarf: Mirage
- Oceanic Coat: Oceanic
- Oceanic Clothes
- Bonding Bridge
- Charnel Boots: One Step in the Grave

SKILLS

Gale Slash | Defense Break | Inspire | Down Attack | Power Attack | Switch Attack | Pinpoint Attack | Combo Blade V | Martial Arts VIII | Fire Magic III | Water Magic III | Wind Magic III | Earth Magic III | Dark Magic III | Light Magic III | Strength Boost (L) | Combo Boost (L) | MP Boost (L) | MP Cost Down (L) | MP Recovery Speed Boost (L) | Poison Resist (S) | Gathering Speed Boost (S) | Dagger Mastery X | Magic Mastery III | Dagger Secrets III | Affliction VIII | Presence Block III | Presence Detect II | Sneaky Steps I | Leap V | Quick Change | Cooking I | Fishing | Swimming X | Diving X | Shearing | Superspeed | Ancient Ocean | Chaser Blade | Jack of All Trades | Sword Dance | Shed Skin | Web Spinner VIII | Ice Pillar | Subzero Domain | Nether Nexus | Cataclysmic Eruption | Water Wielding VI | Substitute

TAMED MONSTER

Name Oboro A fox with skills that bewilder foes

Fleeting Shadow | Shadow Clone | Binding Barrier | etc.

NewWorld Online Status — GUILD **Maple Tree**

NAME Chrome   **LV** 87
HP 940/940   **MP** 52/52

PROFILE
The Unstoppable, Unyielding Zombie Tank

Known as a top player since the early days of *NewWorld Online*. Reliable, caring, everyone's big brother. Like Maple, he's a Great Shielder. His unique gear gives him a 50 percent chance of surviving any hit with 1 HP, and he has a ton of healing skills that make him extremely tenacious.

STATUS
STR 140   **VIT** 185   **AGI** 040
DEX 030   **INT** 020

EQUIPMENT
- Headhunter: Life Eater
- Wrath Wraith Wall: Soul Syphon
- Bloodstained Skull: Soul Eater
- Bloodstained Bone Armor: Dead or Alive
- Robust Ring
- Impregnable Ring
- Bonding Bridge

SKILLS
Thrust · Elemental Blade · Shield Attack · Sidestep · Deflect · Great Defense · Taunt · Bulwark · Impregnable Stance · Iron Body · Guardian · Heavy Body · HP Boost (L) · HP Recovery Speed Boost (L) · Cover · MP Boost (L) · Green's Grace · Great Shield Mastery X · Defense Mastery X · Cover Move X · Multi-Cover · Pierce Guard · Counter · Guard Aura · Defensive Formation · Guardian Power · Great Shield Secrets IX · Defense Secrets VIII · Burn Resist (L) · Stun Nullification · Paralyze Nullification · Poison Nullification · Sleep Nullification · Freeze Nullification · Mining IV · Gathering VII · Shearing · Spirit Light · Indomitable Guardian · Battle Healing · Reaper's Mire · Crystallization · Stimulation

TAMED MONSTER
Name Necro — An armor monster that really shines when worn

Polterguard · Impact Reflection · etc.

NewWorld Online Status

GUILD **Maple Tree**

NAME Iz **LV** 71
HP 100/100 MP 100/100

PROFILE
The Ultimate Crafter

A specialized crafter, she's proud of her work and particular about the results. Her gaming style is all about making clothes, weapons, armor, and items. Originally, she wasn't that active in combat, but her stock of attack and support items now makes a huge difference.

STATUS
- STR 045
- VIT 020
- AGI 090
- DEX 210
- INT 085

EQUIPMENT
- Blacksmith Hammer X
- Alchemist Goggles: Faustian Alchemy
- Alchemist Long Coat: Magic Workshop
- Blacksmith Leggings X
- Alchemist Boots: New Frontier
- Potion Pouch
- Item Pouch
- Bonding Bridge

SKILLS
Strike · Crafting Mastery X · Crafting Secrets X · Enhance Success Rate Boost (L) · Gathering Speed Boost (L) · Mining Speed Boost (L) · Crafting Quantity Boost (L) · Crafting Speed Boost (L) · Affliction III · Sneaky Steps V · Keen Sight · Smithing X · Sewing X · Horticulture X · Synthesizing X · Augmentation X · Cooking X · Mining X · Gathering X · Swimming VII · Diving VIII · Shearing · Godsmith's Grace X · Observer's Eye · Attribute Endowment VII · Botany · Mineralogy

TAMED MONSTER
Name Fey — A spirit that helps with item creation

Item Boost · Recycle · etc.

NewWorld Online Status

GUILD Maple Tree

NAME Kasumi **LV** 84
HP 435/435 **MP** 70/70

PROFILE
The Solitary Sword Dancer

A katana-wielding female player with a strong knack for solo play. Always calm, she's good at assessing the big picture. Yet she's frequently left reeling by Maple's and Sally's outlandish antics. Has a range of katana skills that let her contribute to almost any combat situation.

STATUS
STR 205 **VIT** 080 **AGI** 115
DEX 030 **INT** 030

EQUIPMENT
- Yukari, the All-Consuming Blight
- Cherry Blossom Barrette
- Cherry Blossom Vestments
- Edo Purple Hakama
- Samurai Greaves
- Samurai Gauntlets
- Gold Obi Fastener
- Cherry Blossom Crest
- Bonding Bridge

SKILLS
Gleam, Helmsplitter, Guard Break, Sweep Slice, Eye for Attack, Inspire, Attack Stance, Katana Arts X, Cleave, Throw, Power Aura, Armor Slicer, HP Boost (L), MP Boost (M), Attack Boost (L), Poison Nullification, Paralyze Nullification, Stun Resist (L), Sleep Resist (L), Freeze Resist (L), Burn Resist (L), Longsword Mastery X, Katana Mastery X, Longsword Secrets VIII, Katana Secrets VIII, Mining IV, Gathering VI, Diving V, Swimming VI, Leap VII, Shearing, Keen Sight, Indomitable, Sword Spirit, Dauntless, Sinew, Superspeed, Ever Vigilant, Mind's Eye, Specter of Carnage

TAMED MONSTER
Name Haku — A white snake that ambushes foes from the mist

Supergiant, Paralytoxin, etc.

I Don't Want to Get Hurt, so I'll Max Out My Defense
Welcome to NewWorld Online

NewWorld Online Status

GUILD: Maple Tree

NAME: Kanade **LV 60**
HP 335/335 MP 250/250

PROFILE
The Whimsical Genius Mage

A certifiable genius with an androgynous look and a memory beyond compare. His mind once left him avoiding human contact, but Maple's innocent cheer broke through that shell. He can store all manner of spells in the grimoires on his book stacks, ready for use in combat.

STATUS
STR 015 VIT 010 AGI 090
DEX 050 INT 135

EQUIPMENT
- Divine Wisdom: Akashic Records
- Diamond Newsboy Cap VIII
- Smart Coat VI
- Smart Leggings VIII
- Smart Boots VI
- Spade Earrings
- Mage Gloves
- Bonding Bridge

SKILLS
Magic Mastery VIII Fast Chant MP Boost (L) MP Cost Down (L) MP Recovery Speed Boost (L)
Magic Boost (L) Green's Grace Fire Magic VII Water Magic V Wind Magic VIII Earth Magic V
Dark Magic III Light Magic VIII Sorcerer's Stacks Reaper's Mire Magic Meld

TAMED MONSTER
Name: Sou A slime that can copy a player's abilities
Mimic Divide etc.

Don't Want to Get Hurt, so I'll Max Out My Defense
Welcome to NewWorld Online

NewWorld Online Status — GUILD **Maple Tree**

NAME Mai LV **54**
HP 35/35 MP 20/20

PROFILE
Conquerer Twin

A beginner player with an extreme attack build, she and her younger twin sister, Yui, were scouted by Maple. She does her best to help everyone out. The twins have the highest DPS in the game, and their dual-wielding hammers vaporize anything that gets close.

STATUS
STR 510 VIT 000 AGI 000
DEX 000 INT 000

EQUIPMENT
- Black Annihilammer X
- Black Doll Dress X
- Black Doll Tights X
- Black Doll Shoes X
- Little Ribbon
- Silk Gloves
- Bonding Bridge

SKILLS
Double Stamp | Double Impact | Double Strike | Attack Boost (L) | Hammer Mastery X
Throw | Farshot | Conqueror | Annihilator | Giant Killing | Destroy Mode | Titan's Lot

TAMED MONSTER
Name **Tsukimi** — A bear monster with distinctive black fur
Power Share | Bright Star | etc.

Don't Want to Get Hurt, so I'll Max Out My Defense
Welcome to NewWorld Online

NewWorld Online Status

GUILD Maple Tree

NAME Yui **Lv** 54

HP 35/35 MP 20/20

PROFILE
Annihilator Twin

A beginner player with an extreme attack build, she and her older twin sister, Mai, were scouted by Maple. She's more positive than Mai and quicker to recover. The twins have the highest DPS in the game. Throwing Iz's custom-made iron balls lets them take out enemies at range.

STATUS
STR 510   VIT 000   AGI 000
DEX 000   INT 000

EQUIPMENT
- White Annihilammer X
- White Doll Dress X
- White Doll Tights X
- White Doll Shoes X
- Little Ribbon
- Silk Gloves
- Bonding Bridge

SKILLS
Double Stamp | Double Impact | Double Strike | Attack Boost (L) | Hammer Mastery X
Throw | Farshot | Conqueror | Annihilator | Giant Killing | Destroy Mode | Titan's Lot

TAMED MONSTER
Name Yukimi — A bear monster with distinctive white fur
Power Share | Bright Star | etc.

Don't Want to Get Hurt, so I'll Max Out My Defense
Welcome to NewWorld Online

Prologue

The seventh stratum was enormous, but the more they explored, the less uncharted territory it held. Then the ninth event had them hunting new types of monsters—fish swimming through the air, and monsters with water attacks spawning everywhere. All members of the Maple Tree guild did their part to increase the total kill count.

Since they had to kill a lot of these monsters, they weren't that difficult; none of our heroes really struggled. But the monsters' attack patterns were novel and they could move freely through the air, so plenty of players struggled to target them. Maple could shoot anything down, whether her targets were airborne or not, so she wasn't affected.

Monsters killed by any players in the game were added to the total kill count, and it soon became clear they'd easily reach the goal long before the event ended—even if Maple Tree didn't really dedicate themselves to the task. Maple chose to kick back and relax, enjoying things her way, and deepening her ties with her new friends in Thunder Storm and Rapid Fire.

But once the target was achieved, the event reached a new

stage. This was why it lasted so long. From that day forth, giant monsters—raid bosses—began to spawn, with HP so high even Maple's crew could not tackle them on their own.

Fortunately, after some very specialized training, Mai and Yui now wielded eight hammers each. With the twins' offense at the core, Maple Tree teamed up with the Order of the Holy Sword, Flame Empire, Thunder Storm, and Rapid Fire to take down these raid bosses.

Out on her own, Maple found a significant-looking item—and with that, they left the vast seventh stratum behind and headed for the eighth.

The new map was covered in water, leaving the customary sights now deep below the surface. Exploration here would clearly be a very different experience. Maple's eyes feasted on the horizon and the tops of buildings that just crested the surface, wondering what might be out there.

CHAPTER 1

Defense Build and the Diving Suits

Crossing bridges strung between the sunken buildings, they made their way to the eighth-stratum Guild Home. Portions of it were flooded; a staircase plunged into the water, as if inviting them to dive in.

"Is it safe to go down?"

"It's part of the Guild Home, so I doubt it'll be dangerous… I could scout it for you?"

Sally was good at swimming, so she stepped in—and a window popped up informing her it was currently impossible to enter.

"Or not, I guess. That phrasing makes it sound like there's a condition we haven't cleared yet."

There was still much about this area they didn't understand; best to explore a while first. Sally double-checked the admin notes. Since they'd hit the target in the last event, they should have unlocked something that would help them out here.

"I bet that's related."

"Let's go explore!" Maple cried.

Like they always did, they split up to scope out the town. Most of it was underwater; there were NPCs moving around on boats.

Exploration by foot was restricted to the bridges strung between the buildings.

Maple and Sally paired up and left the Guild Home to explore the eighth-stratum town.

"Can we go in the buildings that are underwater?"

"Good question. It seems like they're pretty far down."

The water itself was clear, so they could see the buildings the surface structures were built on. Like Sally said, the town had repeatedly built on what came before, and the foundations went deep.

"Based on what it looks like outside of town, the water just goes on forever—there's gotta be a way to explore underwater."

Otherwise, the floor would be quite tiny, limited to the area around the tops of the buildings. Neither of them thought that seemed likely—and they didn't have to walk long before they found the answer on sale.

This store was a lot like the shops on the third floor that sold flying machines. It offered all kinds of diving suits, just begging players to use them to explore.

"Let's take a look."

"Sure!"

As they browsed, an NPC came up to them.

"If you want to venture below the waves, diving suits are essential! And depending on the treasures you bring back, you'll be able to descend farther."

A window popped up in front of them—a message from the admins.

The diving suits had been unlocked early and would help them explore the depths. Combined with the drops from the previous event, they could dive deeper. Finding the gear waiting on the ocean floor was the primary goal of this stage.

"So you keep diving, collecting parts to boost the suits, go even deeper, and hunt for rare gear. I bet if we upgrade these, we'll be able to reach the lower levels of our Guild Home, too."

"Whoa… If the water's this deep, there must be all kinds of stuff down there!"

"Treasures waiting in sunken ships? Then it's a salvage operation!"

Buildings lost to the waves, remnants of a lost civilization… Sally might well have been right—these depths most certainly hid all sorts of treasure. And if this was a staged progression like the fourth floor's gates, it was probably a good idea to move fast.

"Let's buy some!"

"And then take them for a test dive."

"Agreed!"

Maple and Sally each picked out a suit and headed into the field—which was mostly open water, with nary a foothold in sight.

Sally helped Maple onto a boat and rowed out across the ocean. Like the fourth stratum, the eighth was progression-gated; they'd have to upgrade their new diving suits before they could dive all that far. The instructions said if they tried diving past the suit's limits, their dive time limit would rapidly drop. To upgrade, they'd need to salvage materials hidden in the shallows, then use the upgraded suits to reach deeper zones.

"It really is a whole ocean!"

"Mm-hmm, and with no land, there's no monsters roaming around. Exploring here should feel real different."

"I'm not great at swimming, but I'm gonna find what I can!"

The diving suits and the underwater exploration items they'd found in the last event were just boosters.

Unlike Sally, Maple didn't have the Diving or Swimming

skills, so she couldn't spend nearly as much time underwater and was nowhere near as mobile. She'd have to take her time, gather upgrade parts, and extend her dive time.

At this point, they didn't know what it was like down there, so they stayed close to town, picking an area they could access with the default diving suits.

Sally stopped rowing there and put on her suit. Diving suits didn't count as equipment, but they did change your appearance; instead of her usual blue outfit, Sally was now wearing a wet suit. It boosted her agility but didn't extend her dive time much. A good fit for Sally's speedy build.

"I look different but…yup, my gear's unaffected."

"I think that's a first! Other equipment made us change."

"Well, we *are* in a proper field, so it could be pretty rough if we lost our equipment skills and stats. If they're gonna take this approach moving forward, there's a chance we can use that…"

If Maple didn't look like she was in her usual black armor, she might be capable of using skills her opponents didn't expect. The diving suits were exclusive to the eighth stratum, making this more of a future concern than anything else.

Either way, they were here to explore. Maple put on her own diving suit. She'd chosen a full-body suit, like an astronaut's; it even had an oxygen tank strapped to the back. The face mask was translucent, so Sally could still make out her expressions.

Unlike Sally's suit, this one allowed her to stay underwater a long time—but the default mobility was decidedly subpar. Her plan was to ignore speed and just slowly walk around down there.

"Oh, now that I've got it on, this feels like the real deal!"

"Yeah?"

"I bet I can stay down for ages!"

"Cool, then let's dive in and find out!"

"Good plan. On three?"

"Go for it!"

As one, they leaped into the water. Bubbles rose, obscuring their vision. When they could see again, they found themselves in a clear blue expanse, surrounded by dilapidated buildings—an underwater ruin. There were regular old fish swimming around, aquatic plants swaying, and also a couple of monsters. None of them seemed particularly interested in the two girls, but still worth keeping an eye on.

"How you doing, Maple?"

"Wahhh! Sally?"

They were underwater, but Sally's voice sounded normal. Maple had only skimmed the suit's description, so she didn't realize this was a standard diving suit function.

"The whole floor is like this, so they decided to keep communication simple. Would be hard to explore otherwise."

"Oh, that makes sense. Kinda weird, though…"

"Keep an eye on your dive limit. But let's look around. Moving is definitely harder than usual."

They could talk freely, but they were still underwater; getting around required swimming.

"At least it seems like these monsters don't attack unless we go after them first. Let's check out these buildings."

"Okay!"

They couldn't surface quickly from inside the ruins, so it made sense to explore the interior while they had more breathing room. Sally led the way, slipping inside the submerged building. The doors and window glass were long gone, so entry was easy; they were soon scouring every corner.

The rooms themselves were devoid of furnishings. Instead, there was seaweed with tiny fish living inside, and giant clams.

"Not seeing any treasure chests."

"We're only a few meters down. Those might be a ways off."
"Can't wait!"
"Then we'll have to find these suit boosters."
They pushed through the weeds, looking for anything of the sort.
"Sally, I found stairs!"
"Let's go down. From the outside, it looked like we can always bail through a window if something goes wrong."

The structure looked as though the inhabitants had built more floors on top as the old ones flooded. That meant the stairs, windows, and doors weren't really placed where they'd be in a regular house. Every floor could become a basement once the waters got high enough, so it made sense they'd have lots of stairs and exits.

The floor they were on had likely sunk fairly recently, so the stairs went down a long way.

"Yeah! We'll be fine even if monsters come at us."
"……just don't use any poison, okay? It'll spread through the water."
"O-oh! Good point."

Maple had used that to defeat the giant squid in the second event, but if she poisoned the water around them here, it would be a disaster. Any monsters entering the area would be slaughtered, true—but so would plenty of players, Sally among them. Maple had no way of neutralizing the poison, so it could be catastrophic.

It was better to use Paralyze Shout, which worked quickly and left no toxic residue.

They were careful, and encountered no real issues, so they dove deeper in search of upgrade materials. Even with default diving suits, they could explore a single building without difficulty. Several floors down, they found something sparkling in the seaweed. It wasn't reflecting light; rather, it was glowing to be eye-catching.

"Sally, over there!"

Maple was more walking than swimming toward it. She reached into the weeds, and found a blue glowing orb and a mechanical-looking nut and bolt.

"Those do seem like materials…but what's this?"

"Probably also what we're looking for. You know how in the last event, monsters dropped those water orbs?"

Sally let Maple claim the spoils, and they read the descriptions together.

"Mm-hmm, see, all materials."

"Will the others glow like this?"

"I'm betting they do. Too soon to be sure, but that didn't look random. This should help speed things up."

If they had to surface every few minutes, the eighth stratum would take far too long to explore—the diving suits were designed to give players plenty of time, even if someone had Maple's stats. Still, she was not built for swimming and definitely felt like she was at a disadvantage. It made her extra happy they'd found some materials so soon. Improving the diving suits would help compensate for stat shortcomings.

"We should have time to find at least one more!"

"Then let's keep going. But let's be careful so we don't accidentally drown."

"Yeah, that might be the toughest part of this floor…"

Losing track of their time limit and drowning unexpectedly would be no fun. This water was like the lava they'd encountered before—once again, Maple's greatest threats came from terrain.

While Maple and Sally were diving, Iz and Kasumi were trying a different sector.

Sally might have raised her Swimming and Diving skills higher than anyone else in Maple Tree, but Iz was actually the second best.

Kasumi had the skills, too, so they'd decided they could match each other's pace. That left Chrome, Kanade, Mai, and Yui exploring elsewhere. The eighth stratum's fields were very different from the lower levels and placed emphasis on entirely different skills.

Iz was planning on gathering aggressively, so she chose a diving suit that let her stay down longer. Kasumi matched Sally's choice, prioritizing mobility.

They hopped in a boat and rowed out across the infinite expanse. Well…Iz was the one who made the boat, so they didn't actually have to row.

"……does it have…an engine?"

"Technically, no, but close enough. Haven't really had much use for it, but I'm glad I had one crafted and in stock."

What *looked* like a boat was speeding across the waves, kicking up spray in its wake. It was more like a Jet Ski than a boat.

"You need DEX to steer, so Maple, Mai, and Yui would have trouble, sadly."

"It's a big floor. Having one of these for everyone would certainly help out. Too bad."

"I'm gonna start by gathering as many materials as I can. That should help improve everyone's progress."

She'd get more materials in the long run if she focused on gathering what they needed to upgrade everyone's diving suits now.

"That sounds good."

"In return, I'll need you salvaging treasures from the depths. I'm counting on you!"

In the shallows, few monsters were aggressive—but that probably wouldn't be the case deeper down. At some point, combat skills were going to become more important than gathering ones.

From that point on, it would be hard for Iz to play a big role. She could fight a little but was primarily a crafter.

After a lengthy ride, Iz stopped her Jet Ski.

Shallows were mostly located around the town, but they could also be found all over the map. There wasn't really a need for them to have gone out this far, but doing so meant they had the place to themselves.

"This way we can explore stress-free and clean the place out."

"Yes, you handle the gathering. I'll focus on monsters. They'll likely be stronger out here."

Kasumi didn't have many gathering skills, so it would be more efficient if Iz handled all of that. Kasumi would be her bodyguard.

"Then let's dive!"

"Ready when you are."

They put on their diving suits, got off the Jet Ski, and dove into the water. They soon figured out exactly what the deal was with shallows far from town.

"Aha… That explains it."

"This was a mountain, once."

Below them was a rocky slope. The small island atop the waves had once been the mountain peak.

"If we look carefully, we might find a cave."

"Yeah, might even count as a dungeon. Still…those are more likely to be deeper down."

They'd have to upgrade their diving suits to the right level before doing anything else.

"Interesting! I bet we'll find neat things."

If this region had been a mountain, then perhaps other areas had been plains, or had even started out underwater to begin with. All kinds of dungeons lay undiscovered beneath this oceanic expanse.

"Really feels like uncharted territory."

"But to get there first, we've gotta grind hard."

"Exactly. Oh, I bet I can mine there."

Iz grabbed her pickax and pointed out the place to Kasumi. Materials weren't gonna gather themselves while they stood around talking. There were several gathering spots on the mountain's surface as well as several glowing points like the one Maple had found.

"I'll take out nearby monsters. You focus on your thing, Iz."

"Thanks. Don't mind if I do!"

Iz swam off, and the large fish circling them turned to follow her.

"Armored Arms."

Kasumi used one of her favorite skills, summoning two disembodied arms. She bolted forward, catching up with Iz, and swung her blade as she activated another skill.

"Blood Blade."

This was designed to attack multiple foes at once, liquefying her sword as she slashed horizontally.

"Good, I can use it underwater."

It didn't spread out the way Maple's poison did—it just followed its usual path, slicing all the fish in half. If the attack worked as she expected, then she could take advantage of the mobility that swimming gave her.

Kasumi turned upward, swimming above the school of fish, then cracked her Blood Blade downward like a whip. From up here, she had no blind spots—a positional advantage that would have been all too fleeting on the surface, but here it allowed her to methodically work her way through the mob. It was very one-sided.

"Didn't even need Armored Arms."

Once the last fish vanished, she scanned the horizon, then swam back to Iz's side.

"Thanks, Kasumi. I *can* use bombs underwater, but they're not nearly as strong."

Explosives were Iz's default means of attack. If those were ineffective, she preferred to avoid combat entirely.

"Not to worry. Doesn't seem like any monsters this close to the surface pose a threat."

"Good to hear."

Iz hit the gathering spot with her pickax. Mining here gave her the usual ores and a chance at diving suit upgrade materials—which were the same odds for gathering rare materials. Naturally, those odds were improved by her gathering enhancement skills—so much that this was actually more efficient than going for the glowing points.

"Wow... I guess that's the power of specialization."

"You bet. I'll gather enough for everyone!"

She could make promises like that because she'd poured a ton of hours into leveling her gathering and crafting skills.

"I'm gonna practicing moving underwater."

"Good idea. What you need to do in a pinch is so different down here."

The trick to underwater combat was being able to deal with attacks from all directions. At this level, monsters mostly charged straight ahead, but in the near future, they'd be fighting monsters with skills of their own. Best to get the hang of fighting underwater now.

"We can both stay down a while, Iz. Let's check how deep we can go."

"Okay. You never know—we might find something worthwhile."

They spent a long time gathering on the submerged mountain.

Unaware that Iz even had a Jet Ski, the remaining four members of Maple Tree were exploring close to town, much like Maple and Sally. They'd avoided areas with lots of sunken buildings, instead

choosing an open, sandy area. Like the mountain, this was a slope, descending so deep they couldn't see the bottom; it wasn't really a beach but more like the side of a hill.

"Okay, no risk of ambushes here."

"Right. There's actually more monsters because of that, but it's easier to handle if we can see them coming."

Mai and Yui would die if either of them took a single hit, and none of them were good swimmers, so this team was not built for underwater exploration. They'd picked this spot with that in mind.

"This'll let you use that safety strat of yours. Should we dive in?"

""Okay!""

Given their builds, having enhanced mobility wouldn't do much for this quartet, so all of them had picked diving suits that extended the duration of their dives. They dove in, the twins already implementing their survival strategy.

"……Good. I was a bit scared it would create a whirlpool."

"Doesn't seem like they implemented anything like that. Otherwise, it would be hard to swing your weapons around underwater."

Mai and Yui's plan was something they'd recently come up with to help them get around any map. Specifically, they would use Helping Hands to spin six extra hammers in a circle around them and automatically pulverize any monsters that got close.

This would not really be effective against other players, but many monsters just charged blindly in—so it worked wonders there. Chrome had seen forum posts discussing sightings of mystery black and white tornadoes, and knew just who they were talking about.

"We'll have to stay clear of that."

"Yeah, that would be instant death—well, not actually. But it *will* send us flying."

There was no friendly fire, so the hit wouldn't damage them—but the sheer momentum would knock them around. Sally had

once used that mechanic to launch Maple upward, but this would probably be far worse.

Still, the strategy kept the twins safe from harm. Chrome and Kanade merely had to keep an eye out for any monsters nimble enough to slip past the whirling hammers, as unlikely as that was.

"We'll start gathering—you two should stay in range of Cover Move, though."

""Will do!""

Hammers spinning, Mai and Yui moved around, picking up materials. Taking care not to bump into them, Chrome and Kanade did their own gathering.

"Don't think we're getting enough to hit up a dungeon today, but the faster the better."

"Every bit counts. I don't mind the grind, myself."

"Yeah, it's kinda therapeutic."

Chrome had found his gear as a result of exactly that kind of slow and steady play, so Kanade's opinion hit home. They were both happily gathering upgrade parts.

"Still, I've never explored underwater. Feels like it'll take some getting used to."

"The twins are way ahead of us."

Kanade glanced up to find them cheerily strolling across the ocean floor, annihilating any innocent monsters in their way.

"I dunno if that counts as getting 'used to' anything."

"Fair."

"But the next event might require underwater combat. Maybe worth picking up the Swimming skill…"

"Could be vital. I figure the skill will level itself while we're on this stratum."

"True."

As they talked and gathered, the twins called out.

"Chrome! Can we go that way?"

"We've already gathered everything here."

"Sure! Don't worry, we're watching your backs."

""Thank you so much!""

They made sure they stayed in range, but the twins were now so strong Chrome had to wonder if they even needed his protection.

◆□◆□◆□◆□◆

Everyone spent a while gathering parts, then regrouped at the Guild Home.

Maple and Sally were back first, soon followed by the Chrome crew.

"We got quite a few! We poked around the sunken buildings, and it seemed like there were multiple parts hidden in every building."

"Yeah? Ours were scattered about the sand, so they were easy to spot. Only real problem is the competition."

Much like the fourth stratum's gradual expansion, everyone would have to gather enough parts to delve deeper. Like Chrome had said, it was all about the grind.

But then they heard a *vroom*, and the boat-shaped Jet Ski pulled up in front of the Guild Home. Iz and Kasumi stepped off.

"Oh, we're the last to arrive?"

"W-we went pretty full throttle, too…"

"…What is that thing?"

"A boat!"

"You make the weirdest things."

"I don't think you've got the DEX to ride it, Chrome."

"I wouldn't dream of it! I'd just flip over."

"Um, banter is good and all, but we've actually gathered a ton of parts."

"Wow, that *is* a lot."

Iz showed off her haul, and it was more than what the other two parties had gathered combined.

"Gosh, nice work, Iz!"

"That's incredible. So many in no time at all."

"We were the only ones who headed that far out. It does seem like the gathering spots give more parts the farther from town you are."

The farther from base you got, the stronger the monsters were. Naturally, that meant the rewards were also richer.

"Distant shallows…"

"More of an underwater mountain."

"I'd imagine the original ground level is much deeper down. The part we've got access to now is basically all mountaintops."

"And it's safe to assume that salvageable treasures are all in the deepest sectors."

"If we all gather this many parts a few more times, we should be able to upgrade one suit enough to dive deeper."

There were several types of suit upgrades, encompassing everything from boosting stats to increasing dive time. One of these upgrades allowed the wearer to access deeper waters. If they only went for that, and pooled the resources everyone had gathered, they could easily upgrade a single suit.

"Having all of us search the shallows is fine, too, but don't you wanna know what lies beyond that *right now*?"

"Well, yeah."

In which case, whose suit should they upgrade? Everyone knew the answer and was looking her way.

"Wait…me?"

"Yep! I figure you're the best candidate, Sally."

Everyone agreed with Maple—even Iz, who'd expected just

this outcome when she'd suggested it. No one was going to argue that point.

"You've got the highest underwater skills and top-tier combat powers. This is all you."

"……Okay, then. If I can get parts from all of you, I'll explore enough to pay that back."

With Sally on board, Maple Tree had a plan of action. Send Sally out ahead, and if she could gather more parts there, that would benefit the entire guild. The more dangerous the location, the better the loot.

"Eh-heh-heh! A big responsibility, Sally."

"I know. I swear I'll bring back results."

"And I wanna see what's down those stairs into the Guild Home."

"True. Seems like we've gotta upgrade the diving suits to go down there."

"The first time they've ever locked us out of our own homes!"

"What could be hiding in there?"

The eighth stratum had only just launched, and nobody knew anything about it yet. But Maple's friends were hard at work, eager to discover what treasures awaited them.

A few days later, Iz's estimate panned out, and they'd gathered enough parts for Sally's suit to operate one level deeper. As planned, Sally upgraded her suit, and then headed for the Guild Home stairs.

"I'm gonna scope this out. It *is* in town, so I doubt there'll be monsters."

But they'd seen nothing like this before, so it didn't hurt to be careful.

Sally took a deep breath, then headed down the flooded staircase. The room below looked a lot like the ruins she'd explored, and there were more rooms leading out of it.

Sally kept a dagger in one hand, watching her surroundings as she moved. In one room, she found a set of stone shelves lined with slabs.

"They can't put books underwater, so we've got these instead?"

Some were clearly older than others. The writings on them described how the water levels had begun to rise, where the water had come from, and how this stratum had come to be.

"I bet the water source is gonna be a dungeon. And this…is in code?"

Several of the slabs were filled with unreadable ciphers, and Sally wasn't sure what to make of that. But many of the things she'd found here seemed like clues leading her to places where good stuff was hidden.

"I guess that's it. Can I go deeper…? Not yet."

A few flights down, she found herself restricted again, and turned back. It seemed like the Guild Home's lower floors mostly provided hints. The eighth stratum was much harder to explore without planning ahead, so these would certainly offer useful guidance.

Since it was in town, there were no monsters, and Sally safely returned to the world above.

"How was it, Sally?"

"Stone slabs in place of books, with what seemed like hints about dungeon locations. Several of them were in code and I couldn't read them, but they might be maps?"

"I see. If we follow those clues, we can hit up the best spots quickly."

"With deeper dungeons, you'll want to take the shortest route to them, or you'll waste dive time."

"So I'll just share all this with everyone."

Sally sent around the photos she'd taken, and set plans for the day.

"If I'm reading this right, the next layer down should have some dungeons, or at least events leading to rare items. I'm gonna look around for those while I gather parts."

"Got it! Take care, Sally!"

"If it's too risky, just retreat. It's hard to fight underwater."

It wouldn't be all that long before the rest of the guild could join her. If the threat level was high enough that she couldn't handle a regular boss on her own, then she might as well wait until all eight suits were upgraded.

"Let's hope the number of parts increases."

"If it does, you're next up for an upgrade, Iz. That'll speed this whole thing up."

Sally would be there with her, so she'd have all the backup she needed. The real stratum exploration would begin when all their diving suits were fully upgraded. It would take a long time before they reached what had once been the surface.

"I'll keep helping with materials, but I'm also gonna scope out the town a bit," Kanade said. "We've all been focused on the underwater areas so far. If I find anything, I'll let you know—can't do much fighting on my own."

"Oh? With your grimoires…"

"Heh-heh…I'm trying to rebuild my stock. Could come up empty, so don't hold your breath."

But it sounded like he had plans beyond a simple stroll. It was hard to imagine Kanade doing anything without good cause.

The rest of the guild would mostly be focused on upgrade gathering, getting themselves ready for the next area, and the rare items and skills it might contain.

The dev team were busy checking to make sure this new map was functioning correctly—after all, they'd never had a place with this much water before. They all sounded relieved.

"Whew, thank goodness."

"How are the players approaching it?"

"Uh...pretty much as planned, thankfully."

"......Has that *ever* happened before?"

"Come to think of it..."

"We've got absolutely tons of one-time events hidden everywhere—these 'treasures.'"

Far below the surface of the waters, on what had once been dry land, there were miniquests and dungeons galore. Salvaging these unique treasures fit the water theme, so the devs had made far more than they usually did and scattered them far and wide. Without luck and instinct, though, it was entirely possible to not find any, and wind up diving and resurfacing with nothing to show for it.

"Some of those are pretty crazy."

"W-well, no telling who'll find them. Could be someone finds something that plays into their build and gets much stronger overnight."

Everyone had a shot at good items and skills. After that, it was up to the luck of the draw.

"That's the thing. The bigger guilds are gonna get there faster and find a bunch."

"They've got the numbers. The more players they have diving, the more likely they are to get lucky."

"That's...part of the design, but..."

Everyone here could think of one guild that just wouldn't apply to.

"They find everything."

"They're on the same wavelength!"

"Like a gallery of rare skills..."

"Maple Tree's salvage operation... Let's hope they don't go overboard."

This was wildly optimistic, and reality soon came knocking.

"Wait, she already picked up the thing, right? From the eighth-stratum monster we slipped in ahead of time."

"It was a rare drop from a creature with a low spawn rate, but that stuff just doesn't matter when it comes to her."

"Gotta chalk it up to luck, but at this rate they'll hoover all the best stuff up."

"Not all of it! They've gotta leave some!"

"But they'll definitely get one or two..."

Like the dev team was saying, this was a treasure hunt—there were rare events, skills, and items hidden among the offerings. More than any of the previous floors. Maple had a proven track record of stumbling across these things, and it was hard not to see her salvage efforts resulting in further headaches.

"It's not just Maple! This is a challenge for everyone! Even with the diving suits, most players aren't great at handling the water yet. It's gonna be a while before anyone starts treasure hunting in earnest."

"Lots of them are thoroughly hidden. Even with hints..."

"Hopefully they enjoy the thrill of the hunt."

"Let's hope, yeah."

"Show us your tracking skills, players!"

Just as the players looked forward to what they'd find, the developers looked forward to seeing players conquer the depths.

CHAPTER 2
Defense Build and New Power

The guild had pooled their parts to let Sally dive deeper, so she rowed her boat out to a location she'd deemed worth checking out.

"If I can ride one, I should have her make me a Jet Ski."

These rowboats were much slower than the seventh stratum's horses, and Sally was feeling the need for speed. These had been fine when she was just chilling with Maple, but now that she was solo, she preferred the efficiency the Jet Ski would afford her. Iz had mentioned a DEX requirement; if she met it, she'd definitely want to upgrade.

"Maybe next time."

For now, she was almost at her destination. Putting the Jet Ski out of her mind, Sally donned her diving suit and dove in. There were rocky overlapping mountains right below her that had once been a regular mountain ridge. It felt like she was looking down at it from the sky.

"Wow, that's bigger than I thought. I think it'll be around here somewhere…"

The map in the Guild Home's basement had shown a mark here. And the terrain below her certainly looked like there was something hidden nearby.

"Okay, gotta start looking. Let's dive deeper."

She'd made her observations, and now it was time to swim on down. There were no monsters near the surface, but they started showing up as she neared the rocks below.

"They're aggressive, too!"

Several sharks shot toward her. She'd seen sharks like this a bunch in the ninth event, but that had been on land, and she'd had the advantage. Now the tables were turned—familiarity did not mean she could afford to underestimate them. While she'd been under Maple's protection, Sally had done a lot of checks to see which skills operated differently underwater. Ice Pillar, for instance—this normally made ice grow from the ground. But when the ground was out of sight, she couldn't use the skill at all.

That said, Sally's strength was not especially skill-dependent. She was definitely one of the better underwater fighters around, and as long as she kept an eye on her dive time, she could probably handle most challenges.

"Hah! Yah!"

She dodged the shark's water breath attacks—they'd changed the color of them to make them stand out, even underwater—and raked the monsters with her daggers in passing. Sword Dance boosted her attack, while Chaser Blade, Whet Wisp, and Water Cowl all upped the damage—so regular attacks were now far more devastating than they had been in her last underwater brawl, from before she'd obtained any of her current gear.

"Skill compatibility isn't all that great, but it's still hitting nice and hard."

The fire element was much less effective underwater, and water didn't do much against water-themed enemies. The fact that she was doing this much damage likely came down to her maxed-out Sword Dance attack buff. The requirements for it were strict, so it paid out accordingly.

Sally threaded her way through the sharks, destroying one after another. If they were still just using breath attacks, they posed no threat to her, even underwater. The dungeon boss she'd obtained her unique series from had been far tougher.

"And that's the last of 'em!"

She kicked hard, darting forward, and sliced up the last shark, coming to a stop in the water.

"All that Water Wielding means I can move better than I thought."

Unlike the others, she had Swimming and Diving maxed, plus Iz's underwater support items and the eighth stratum's diving suit. Unlike the fight that had given her a unique series, she didn't really have a meaningful time limit here.

She knew there was no risk of drowning as long as she had a straight shot to the surface, so before the mobs respawned, she headed farther down the slope.

"Okay, huh…lessee…"

Everything that had once lived on this mountain was long gone, so there was no risk of any rewards being hidden in some forest. She could simply swim right down precipices, shortcutting the exploration.

"I hope there's something. A dungeon or…"

Sally kept following the slope, diving deeper and deeper.

Sally searched thoroughly, hoping to find a cave hidden among the rocks. She'd upgraded her diving suit ahead of the curve, and there were plenty of other areas accessible at stage one; this meant there were no other players around, and she'd have to find a likely trigger all on her own.

The hint in the Guild Home had just shown this general location—she didn't have anything more specific to work with. With her skills,

she didn't need to surface for a while yet, and could search efficiently—but that still left a lot of range to cover.

"It really is just a lot of rocks. Which I guess makes stuff easier to spot?"

Taking out monsters that got in her way, she swam on between the mountains—and eventually found a deep fissure halfway down. Curious, she edged closer and saw that it clearly ran deep. This might have been what the hint indicated.

"Okay, let's surface once…"

Rather than dive into the fissure right away, Sally turned and swam straight up. Cresting the water once reset her dive time and allowed her to attack the fissure with a full tank.

"Let's clear this in one…or try to, anyway. Not sure if that'll mean much."

There weren't any other players around. If this was a dungeon, she would likely be the first in. In which case…she might nab a second unique series.

Sally took a deep breath, then plunged straight down, heading right for the fissure and wasting no time. It was already pretty far from the surface, so she had a light source ready to aid her exploration, and could see just fine even inside the fissure.

With rock walls flanking her, Sally swam farther in. The water was clear, and there were no monsters in here; if she searched carefully, she was unlikely to miss anything.

"……There's definitely *stuff*."

The first thing she found was a wall riddled with holes. She knew one of these was the right path, and likely led to a monster—she heightened her focus, examining the array.

"Maybe a fish's nest?"

Dagger in hand in case of an ambush, she started working her way through the holes. She'd been worried they all had monsters,

but so far, she'd found none. The holes went on for a bit before hitting dead ends. Some were wide, some were narrow; each time she hit a dead end, she turned back and dove into another.

The lack of monsters certainly sped things up, so Sally made quick work of the place, crossing off one hole after another. Eventually, in one hole, a blue glowing thing made a beeline toward her; Sally kicked hard, evac-ing to the entrance of the hole. A few moments later, a blue mass like the sharks' breath attacks shot past her.

"Well, that's obvious enough."

There had been nothing like that in the previous holes, which meant this was the *right* one. Sally gingerly peered inside once more.

"Was it…not a monster? Or did it flee farther in?"

The water itself was clear, and she could see nothing moving. But that attack had come from somewhere. Bearing Oboro's Spirited Away in mind, she slipped inside.

On the lookout for sharks or otherwise, she swam down the shaft—and was surprised by what she found.

"A device? Looks like it runs on magic, maybe?"

Sticking out of the wall was what looked like a gun barrel, with a blue glow around it. A trap waiting for intruders—she could see signs that this barrel had fired that glowing orb.

"……Whatever's hidden in the depths might be pretty good, then. They gave us diving suits for a reason. Shame I can't bring *this* home."

Sally was beginning to suspect the treasures of the depth were not merely made of gold. Since the eighth-stratum towns were built on top of lost civilizations, all manner of things might be hidden in these depths.

Excited by the prospect of this, Sally swam farther in. She spotted more blue lights, and this time several shots bore down on her. She had leeway to dodge, and she'd spotted them early—they never stood a chance of hitting her, underwater or not.

Adjusting her position, she twisted her body out of harm's way. She'd expected monsters, but there were still no signs of any—just these glowing projectiles. On she went, wondering what else this shaft had in store for her. Eventually, the narrow passage opened up, and she realized this was yet another ant's nest–style dungeon.

"……A junk heap?"

The space was entirely filled with water, but the base of the chamber was covered in heaps of run-down machine parts. Diving suit upgrade parts were mixed in, but most of the junk was just decorative.

She had plenty of dive time left, and Sally was here to haul away as many materials and/or gear as she could, so she made a thorough search of the junk heap, gathering every last scrap before heading down the next passage.

This ant's nest had either been a storeroom or a dump—it was filled with man-made objects. As Sally moved around, any machines still alive reacted by firing projectiles at her. Perhaps this was why there were no living foes around, she thought, gathering more diving suit parts. Since she was a stage deeper, the number of parts that could be gathered had noticeably increased; that alone made exploring this place worthwhile. With no monsters to worry about and the number of projectiles not terribly high, she had no real need to worry about her time limit—so this was not a challenge for Sally.

Still, it *was* a dungeon, and that would all change once she found the door to the boss room. She'd have to kick her focus into overdrive and try to beat it on her first attempt.

But that was what Sally lived for. She needed new skills or equipment—and was hardly here to just leisurely gather parts.

"Let's hope this pays off…!"

Praying there would be a boss room, Sally slipped between light bullets, swimming deeper in.

* * *

The deeper she got, the more broken machine parts she found, and the more attacks she weathered.

Sally dodged through it all, but in time, she found a different kind of light—a soft glow, drifting in the water. Curious what this was, she approached with caution—and the light slowly changed shape, becoming a big fish, and darted toward her.

"Wind Cutter!"

She sent a quick spell flying to fend it off, but the monster was made of light, and the wind blades fazed right through it. Sally tried dodging to avoid the charge, but it tracked her. Instead, she slipped past it, raking it with her daggers, but made no contact—it felt like they caught only water. No visible damage sparks either.

If she'd had more HP and defense, she might have let it hit her to see if it was even a monster at all, but Sally didn't have that option. She kept dodging the charges, trying to work out how to handle this—but there seemed to be only one solution.

"Just gotta keep dodging till I find something, I guess?"

At the very least, it was still easy enough to evade. She pressed onward, keeping an eye out for anything that might help solve the light fish problem. The way this thing just kept charging was simplistic by eighth-stratum standards—it felt like it was *meant* to be dodged.

Even if you didn't have Sally's evasion skills, most players who came this far could probably handle these attacks.

"But I bet this boss is gonna be a weird one, too."

Dodging the fish, she swam on. Never stopping to evade, just making minimal adjustments as she swam, wasting no time and almost acting like it wasn't even there.

She was dodging projectiles at the same time, which was very like her.

This shaft's design was pretty unusual; nothing much in it besides the light guns and the intangible fish. The layout was less "dungeon" than "junkyard submerged beneath the waves." The farther Sally got, the more she started to wonder if there even was a boss.

"Ugh, more of them?"

She'd been dodging the one phantom fish for a while now, and soon more lights appeared ahead of her, which meant two more fish to worry about.

"If you're adding more of them, give me a way to turn them off!"

They'd followed her much farther than most monsters would, so odds were they were some sort of security system—but she'd yet to figure out a way to disable it. And if she didn't know what to do, there was no use worrying about it—all she could do was keep dodging. Making good use of acceleration and deceleration, she slipped right past their telegraphed charges. Being underwater gave her options and allowed her to dodge in all directions; arguably, she moved more like a fish than these creatures of light did.

Moving up and down in the water, she scoured the heaps of broken junk for suit upgrades and ways to stop the fish—but so far, no luck there.

"Okay, be that way."

It seemed like she was would just have to dodge them all the way back. Sally kicked hard, surging onward.

For a while longer, Sally swam on, followed by a ton of fish. There was a whole school of them now, following her every move; she was past the point of leisurely exploration.

"I've lost count of how many there are!"

When there were only a few, she'd done her best to find a way to get rid of them but hadn't been able to find a surefire way to do it. Since her diving suit was made for underwater mobility, she was

still capable of dodging them, but by this point it was definitely something only Sally could pull off.

Still, her focus was finite, and even she was starting to get pessimistic. Since she couldn't knock them away with her daggers, she had limited evasive options, and that made the task all the harder.

"Gimme a gap...now!"

The intangible fish had been swarming all over this open area, but a charge gave her just enough room to corkscrew through and escape into the next passage. These spaces had their own dangers, of course—they were so narrow that if she stopped moving even once, there was no way she could dodge the fish coming at her from behind.

Instead, she hurtled forward until she saw a barrage of lights coming from up ahead. Much like the school of fish behind her, they blanketed the passage—the only gaps to be seen were those created by the lag in between fish launching themselves at her. That was enough for Sally, however—she didn't even slow down, flinging herself right into the hail of projectiles.

"Whew...!"

Her senses honed to the point where everything seemed to move in slow motion, she threaded through openings where making even the slightest error would end her. But the projectiles were never quite aimed at Sally, as if they were never intended to shoot her down—and she left dozens of shots in her wake. She was just doing what she'd always done—dodging all threats, and swimming onward. She wasn't about to get hit by anything that couldn't *think*.

"Okay, I'm through!"

She emerged from the passage, past the barrage—and found her vision filled by a door that towered over her.

And the fish on her heels all vanished at once. The water was still once more. This was clearly the door to the boss room—she'd finally reached the end.

"Have I got time…? Yup, plenty."

Having this much leeway meant she could take her time and deal with this boss properly—for that reason, Sally chose to tackle it.

"I know I'm stronger than the first time I fought a boss underwater."

What lay in wait for her? Sally closed her eyes for a moment, refreshing her focus—then swam up to the door, opening it and peering in.

The chamber was spherical and fully submerged. Like the rooms before, the bottom was filled with ancient parts and unknown machinery. At present, there was no sign of anything resembling a boss.

"Guess I'll have to go in."

On the lookout for ambushes, Sally swam forward—and a screen buried in the junk heap switched itself on. That made Sally brace herself—and sure enough, an array of gun muzzles forced their way through the junk heaps.

These were clearly not the main act, though. Bright lights were generated all over the room, then merged together. The light coalesced into the figure of a man with the lower body of a fish, holding a spear—and with a boss's HP bar over his head. Sally raised her daggers.

"This one looks solid at least. Some security system."

She'd made it this far, but this was the real battle. Sally could not afford to lose—for the sake of the gear this might earn her, and for the sake of her larger goal.

The boss saw Sally's raised daggers and adjusted its grip on the spear. It swung the weapon in a circle, and intangible fish were generated along that arc. All the gun barrels started to glow.

What happened next was all too predictable. All the things she'd dodged on the way in came at her as one.

* * *

"Seen that already!"

Sally sprang into action, dodging everything at once. Both the fish and projectiles were fast, but all of them had been aimed straight at her current location. In an open space, there was little chance of them hitting her as long as she kept moving and maintained a decent speed. Especially for someone as good as she was.

What she really needed to look out for was what happened when she stopped dodging and attacked, as well as the boss's own actions.

All the bosses so far had several attack patterns, and this one was likely no different. Time was on her side; she could afford to figure out what it did, avoid damage, and wait for a a chance to hit back.

Avoiding the incoming attacks, she watched carefully as the boss began to move. It raised the spear high and swung down hard. This time it wasn't a summons—but Sally's instincts screamed a warning, and she kicked hard, moving as fast as she could. Something shot past her, nicking the end of her scarf.

"A current... Gotta keep *that* in mind."

This boss could control the flow of water. It wasn't clear how long this attack would last, but a current thick enough to swallow her up was now slicing the spherical chamber in half. No guarantees she'd survive getting caught in that. It was hard to spot, and since she needed to maintain her speed to avoid the projectiles, all she could do was try to remember where it was.

"Water Cowl!"

Sally made a mental map of the boss room, always updating the position of the current, planning out where she could safely pass—then darted in closer to the boss.

With the current limiting her mobility, and with no clue how long it would stay in place, she couldn't afford to stick to her initial wait-and-see approach.

She slipped through a barrage of projectiles, past a wave of charging fish, deflected the boss's spear thrust with one dagger, and gouged a deep slice in its shoulder with the other. With this many projectiles in play, Sally had easily reached the maximum Sword Dance buff. Her blow hit far harder than it looked, tearing a clear chunk out of the boss's HP bar.

"Good, I can hurt it."

A new current was generated and began chasing her, but she twisted her body, diving down beneath it. She saw the boss summoning even more intangible fish.

"Cool, keep me motivated."

Kicking up her focus another notch, she calmly handled the constant barrage of projectiles.

Sally had always been slippery, and the more she fought, the more she honed those skills.

She dodged everything the boss threw at her, threading though the smallest gaps and closing in to attack.

She was still playing hit and run, but both the damage she was doing and her range of gambits were far superior to when she'd fought the previous underwater boss.

"Hoo…hyah!"

Dodging attacks from all directions, she slashed at the boss. It was far slower than she was, and its spear could not catch up with her. The high volume of attacks and the environment itself worked in the boss's favor, yet it was the one in trouble.

As time wore on, the boss summoned more fish, but as long as there was room between them, Sally would slip through.

She had never left her enemies many openings to begin with, but now that she could do solid damage without having to resort to skills, she was even harder to hit than before.

As the battle raged on, the merman kept placing currents

around the room, like a net covering the area. The fish and light bullets worked for the boss, however, and they were unaffected by the currents, coming at Sally regardless of the water's flow. The situation was only getting worse, yet Sally's focus never flagged.

"One more…!"

She found a gap in the attacks, slipped between the currents, and came swinging back at the boss in the center. No skills used, minimizing her exposure—an approach that left the boss unable to pin her down. She'd lost count of how many times she'd hit it hard.

As the boss's HP hit the halfway point, Sally backed off, bracing herself for what would come next. This was where most bosses changed up.

"……!"

She'd called it—the boss now entered a new phase. Light gathered, forming a second spear—and motes of light began flowing around the web of currents. That did make them easier to see, but they soon proved this wasn't all good news.

As Sally watched, the light clumps shot out of the current. She bent backward to dodge them, but this wasn't a one-time deal; they soon entered the currents again.

"That's just messed up!"

It seemed like these light clumps were designed to come after her irregularly. Far worse than the fixed turrets on the walls, these were mobile cannons, attacking from every which way. Dodging them would take an even greater toll on her nerves.

But Sally was actually relieved that this new phase was so consistent.

As long as she could still dodge, it didn't matter whether the boss had one weapon or two; her approach would not change. And Sally knew she could pull it off.

She kicked the water once more, surging toward the boss. Light

bullets from either side, fish from dead ahead—with the added projectiles, it was like threading a needle.

"Yeah, but I've seen worse," Sally muttered.

She was through the school of fish already. This required her to not leave even a single pinky toe out of place, but when she fought alongside Maple, Sally was *always* weaving through a storm of projectiles. She'd learned to avoid bullets from behind, so she wasn't about to let anything coming from the front hit her.

To Sally, the smallest of gaps looked like a path to guaranteed safety.

"Keep right on trying—it won't get you anywhere."

She slid in past the boss's flank, hit the brakes to avoid both spears by mere inches, then took full advantage of her underwater mobility to stab the boss in the chest.

Against a foe its projectiles could not hit, the extra spear did the boss no good at all.

Sally had a destination in mind, a level of strength she *had* to achieve. For that reason, she'd raised the limits on her own focus, and her combat skills were far more unreasonable than ever before.

Until its HP ran out, she'd come at the boss again and again, aiming unerringly for her foe. More precision, more lethality.

"Equipment or skills, hand 'em over!"

Shooting through a barrage that was like a rain of light, a blue blur streaked toward the boss—and her final blow cut it down.

As the boss burst into fragments of light, the currents and fish vanished, and the guns fell silent. The strength left Sally's body, and her focus dropped back down to standard levels. She was relieved the fight was over.

She still had time left on her dive, so she relaxed, looking around—and realized the screen that had appeared at the start of the fight was glowing again.

Sally braced herself in case this meant more monsters, but fortunately not—the light coalesced in front of it, spawning a treasure chest.

"Oh, you spawn everything, huh? Anything else? No?"

Sally swam over and tapped the side of the screen, but it had gone black and was now unresponsive. This had been the boss room, so perhaps this machine had been behind it all.

"Welp, let's hope you've got something worthwhile!"

Sally popped open the chest lid—and found exactly what she'd been hoping for.

A dagger with a blade larger than the ones she'd been using. A well-worn gray hooded jacket, with several belts and pockets. A simple choker, and a sturdy-looking pair of pants. That was all—but bits of the gear were glowing, generating distinctive yellow polygons. Probably indicating that these objects, like the boss, had come from that screen.

"What do they do?"

Hopes high, Sally quickly checked their descriptions.

Fabrication Coat
[AGI+30] [DEX+25] [Indestructible]
Skill: Guise

Shapeless Blade
[STR+50] [AGI+20] [Indestructible]
Skill: Shapeshifting

Immaterializer
[DEX+20] [INT+30] [MP+50] [Indestructible]
Skill: Hologram

Corporality Garb
[AGI+40] [STR+30] [DEX+20] [Indestructible]
Skill: Reality Twister

Guise
Changes the name and appearance of skills, spells, and equipment. Actual effects and abilities are unchanged.

Shapeshifting
Changes the weapon type at will. Treated as daggers, with corresponding skills.

Hologram
Generates a replica of a skill or spell used within a set period of time. This only replicates the visual effect and does not actually do anything.

Reality Twister
Select from a list of non-damage-dealing skills like Hologram. Anything generated by that skill will now do damage, but attacks generated otherwise will not.
Effect lasts fifteen seconds. Thirty-minute cooldown.

"Whoa, big stat buffs. And these skills…seem like fun."

Sally read them over again. There were skills on all the gear, every bit as spiky as the other unique series she'd seen. Hard to

say any of them would instantly strengthen the wearer. Only Reality Twister did real damage, but given the cooldown, it would only come into play once a battle. And the description made it sound like even if they didn't do damage, many support skills would not be affected by it regardless.

Still, these had potential. Just watching Kanade in action proved the value of having a wide variety of skills on hand.

If she used them right, they could even turn the tide of battle.

"Very much depends on how clever I am. Gonna have to try things out."

She'd have to brainstorm some ideas ahead of time because she'd never be able to take advantage of these on the fly. These weren't like Maple's skills; merely activating them wouldn't accomplish much.

Sally quickly tried out the effects of her new gear.

"Okay, weapon first."

Sally used Shapeshifting. Light gathered round her daggers, and a moment later the new weapon took shape. She was now holding a spear as tall as she was.

"Aha. Could be useful when I'm using other weapons to help train the twins."

She changed the daggers into a number of other weapons. Greatswords, axes, bows, shields—each gave the weapon a different reach, and felt quite different. But that just fascinated her; she ran through them all. If she could switch up her weapon mid-fight and take advantage of that, it could be a legitimate threat.

A lot more things she'd have to practice, but Sally always enjoyed this sort of thing.

"I'll check out the rest back at the Guild Home. Curious what they look like to everyone else."

She switched her gear back to her original unique series, and headed out of the dungeon and back to the surface before she ran out of air.

Back at the Guild Home, Maple was turning a load of materials over to Iz.

"Oh, Sally! You're back. You dove deeper down, right? How was it?"

"Heh-heh, awesome. First, upgrade parts."

Sally handed over everything she'd gathered on this run.

"Mm-hmm, I figured there'd be more parts deeper in. I'll have to do what I can and get everyone upgraded."

Sally's haul was clearly way more than she'd have managed in the shallows; once again, the faster you could get to deeper locations, the better.

"There was quite a lot inside that dungeon, so well worth going in if you find one."

"Got it. I'll let everyone know."

"You found a dungeon? How was it?"

"Heh-heh-heh, like I said, awesome. Look!"

With that, Sally swapped out her gear, and did a spin, showing it off.

"Wow! That's so different! Badass!"

"I approve. Do they come with skills?"

"Yep. That's one reason I'm back. Maple, can I call in a favor?"

"What, what?"

Sally said she needed help trying out her new skills, so Maple and Iz followed her to the training room.

"Figured your skills would make it easy, Maple."

"......?"

"Heh-heh, now I'm curious."

In the training room, Sally explained the favor.

"Stand back a bit… Now, Maple, use Hydra."

"O-okay! Um, Hydra!"

Maple fired her skill at the wall, and the poisonous deluge turned a swath of the room into a toxic swamp.

"Like that?"

"Yup, now hold your shield and face me."

"……? Uh, all right."

With Iz watching closely, Maple did as Sally said.

"Here goes. Hydra!"

Not a cry they'd heard from Sally before—but that magic circle was certainly purple.

Eyes nearly popping out of their heads, they watched an identical deluge of poison bear down on Maple. It hit her raised shield, but where Devour should have gobbled it up—it passed right through.

"Urp?! ……Huh?"

That had come as a shock, but the poison also went right through her, spattering onto the ground behind.

Maple looked at Sally, baffled, and Sally looked very impressed.

"This skill lets me copy the visuals of recent skills. They're fake, so they don't do damage."

Nor did they burst on contact without damage—this was more like the fish she'd fought. Her Holograms could not even be touched. Iz and Sally both stepped into the poison swamp she'd made but felt nothing at all. Visually, though, it was indistinguishable from the real one Maple had made.

"Wow…it really looks just like mine!"

"There's a decent chance it would really confuse people in a fight. This gear is pure PvP. Doubt it would do much if I used it on monsters."

"They don't really struggle with decisions. Still…that sounds

tricky to pull off. These are skills only someone like you can fully exploit, Sally."

"I've also got a skill that makes these illusions real. Can only use that once a fight."

"Then it's effectively a copy skill."

"That sounds great! You can throw out a real Hydra?"

"Yeah, so we'll have to incorporate that into our teamwork."

"Sure thing! Anything else?"

With that experiment down, Maple came closer, eyes sparkling, wondering what else this gear had to offer.

"The new weapon's nifty, too. Watch this."

Sally's dagger turned to light, taking one form after another.

"Ah! That's no illusion, right?"

"It can take the shape of any weapon. I tried it out on the way back, and it works just fine in combat."

"So you can adjust to the situation, then. Wish I could make a weapon like that..."

It was definitely the sort of thing you only found in unique series. If Iz couldn't craft it, no blacksmith in the game could.

And that meant Sally now had a trick up her sleeve that no one could imitate, and no one had ever seen.

"I won't be using this unless it's just our guild around. If no one knows about it, there's a good chance I can blindside 'em."

It would be difficult to dodge a swing that you thought was coming from a dagger until it suddenly became a greatsword. It was always hard to react to the unpredictable.

"And there's one more thing."

"You're not done yet?! Wow, what else?"

"Watch close. Guise."

Sally's gear was wreathed in light, and when the light cleared, she was back in her usual blue coat and scarf.

"Does it work like Quick Change?"

"Nope. Only the visuals changed. See?"

Sally used Shapeshifting, transforming her dagger. That canceled the disguise on her weapon alone, revealing a gray longsword.

"My, my! Gear can do that? Why can't I make this?! I hope they let me later."

"I can change the names and appearances of skills and magic. For instance…Fire Ball!"

A green magic circle appeared at her feet, and wind blades shot toward the training room dummy. But instead of slicing it to pieces, there was a splash, and the dummy was completely soaked.

"?????"

Maple clearly had no clue what had just happened.

"I used Water Ball, but I changed the skill name to Fire Ball, and the visuals to Wind Cutter."

Despite those changes, the nature of the spell itself remained unchanged, so when it hit its target, it produced a water effect.

"I—I see…"

"Used right, this can really work for me. But I've gotta get the hang of it myself. I've got a few ideas, but they call for all-new approaches."

"Ah-ha-ha… I don't think I'd ever get the hang of it, but I bet you will!"

"That's the plan. Gonna try and figure it out before the next PvP."

"Can't wait. Let me know if you need anything for that. I'll get it ready. Exploration and combat are *both* important."

""Yep!""

To master her newfound powers, Sally began a secret training program where no other players could see.

CHAPTER 3

Defense Build and the Submerged Shrine

A while after that, more and more players were gaining access to the next stage down. Exploration was growing easier—all members of Maple Tree had upgraded their suits.

They were still sending Sally ahead to the next stage but otherwise largely keeping pace with each other.

The eighth stratum was pretty big, but with the strict gating, this was where exploration began in earnest. With that in mind, Kanade stayed in town, diving into the Guild Home itself.

Since there were no monsters here, he moved quickly to the pile of hint slabs Sally had discovered.

"Is this it?"

Sally had shared photos, but it wasn't like getting here was hard; now that his suit was upgraded, he'd decided to check it out firsthand.

Kanade wasn't after the map she'd seen but the slabs written in a cryptic cipher. He went through each in turn, nodding to himself.

"Mm-hmm, examined close-up, I'm even more sure. This is a proper clue."

Where Sally had seen a mysterious code, Kanade's eyes were perceiving actual letters, like he'd done before—it seemed this was one of many hidden elements scattered about the game. Since Kanade had spent a lot of time in the game's libraries memorizing the contents of their book collections, this code wasn't unreadable gibberish, but the same language he'd seen used on previous stratums.

"Heh, I was just entertaining myself, but it might actually pay off."

This was the first time he'd found such a direct hint. While other players had spent time out in the fields, he'd been stuck in town, cooped up in the library. He'd spent less time finding things out in the world or clearing dungeons—but that did leave him better suited to solving this kind of mental exercise.

"The box of wisdom…," he read aloud. "Finally? Heh-heh, well, if not, I can always give it to someone else."

With that, he swam back to the surface. He had a new place in mind, and quickly found a boat and rowed toward his destination.

After a leisurely row, he reached a position that went one stage deeper. Peering over the side, he saw buildings below him like the ones in the town—new buildings stacked on old, like ramshackle towers. No glass in the windows, no doors, and monsters lurking within—seemed like it would take a while to scour.

"Hmm, that's a lot of monsters."

Planning his approach, Kanade reviewed his grimoire stock. Using Sou would lower the power of his spells but not use up the grimoires, which made it easy enough for him to handle mobs.

His time in the library had helped him solve this hint, but it also meant he'd spent far less time out grinding levels. He was definitely underleveled by eighth-stratum standards, and would need to make clever use of Akashic Records and Sorcerer's Stacks to prevail.

"If I could one-shot them all, that would simplify things…

Yeah, if I don't take them down, I'll be in trouble. Better play it safe."

Strategy in mind, he put the boat away and dove into the water below.

"Sou, Mimic, Intercept Sorcery."

His slime transformed into a copy of Kanade and deployed four magic circles around them. These moved with Sou, firing missiles of light at any monsters swimming their way. They unleashed powerful, frequent shots—great against monsters who did minimal dodging and mostly charged in a straight line. Shot volume versus enemy quantity. Since they didn't require manual oversight, they worked perfectly even if Sou was using them.

"It gets cramped indoors, so there's likely fewer monsters there. Oops—Electric Spear!"

Sou was handling crowd control, and anything that got through, Kanade took out with the spells Akashic Records had randomly given him for the day. Sparks appeared in the water, forming a spear in his hand; when he threw that, it took out the monster it hit and also did damage to everything in the vicinity.

"Nice. Gotta keep a grimoire of that."

Simple, easy to use, minimal exposure—well worth keeping around. The skills Akashic Records provided let him fill the bookshelves floating behind him, but those grimoires could only be used once. Taming Sou had been huge—the slime could circumvent that downside.

"Gotta pick the right moments to use them."

Slaughtering the area monsters, Kanade eventually reached a window on the tallest building. He checked his dive time, then headed in. Kanade couldn't stay underwater for super long, and it would never do to drown halfway through the building.

"This could take several dives. But if I'm right…"

If this really was what he sought, Kanade figured it would take quite a bit of time.

Depending on his rate of progress, he might be coming here regularly. For now, he swam through the building's interior, pleased to find fewer monsters there.

The buildings might be highly vertical, but the layouts themselves were not that complex; like building blocks, there were stairs or ladders leading down, down, down, and these were easily found. Kanade made sure not to overlook anything but also worked quickly, mindful of his time limit. As he descended, the look of the rooms changed.

"Ah, shouldn't be long now."

The walls and ceilings were decorated with the same writing on the slabs that had led Kanade to this location. Keeping an eye out for traps, he moved closer, reading them.

"I see… Definitely a hidden secret. Like the previous ones."

He'd never seen anyone else with a grimoire-based fighting style. Like many of this game's best skills, you'd never stumble across them exploring *normally*.

Kanade's goal here was very relevant.

Just like when he'd gained Sorcerer's Stacks, the hint had suggested he'd find something that would upgrade Akashic Record's functionality.

Confirming once again that he hadn't misread the code—and that it was intended to be read this way—Kanade moved to the next room.

It was empty, with no furniture at all—just like any other underwater chamber. But he swam right over to the wall, put his hand on it, and cast a spell.

"Glad I got this today. Electric Spear!"

The bolt spread out across the wall. As Kanade watched, a

cobweb of cracks spread—glowing blue. Then the wall parted, opening like a pair of sliding doors.

"Cool. This is definitely the right place."

A complex trick, a gimmick you'd never find exploring normally—Kanade was sure it was hiding something. He swam right on in.

"Next…this way."

To Kanade's eyes, they might as well have scrawled the instructions on the wall in giant letters. If you got past the deciphering phase, the hints weren't that hard to parse. He easily found the hidden passages placed in the stone building's walls, ceilings, and floors.

And Kanade remembered every step of his route here, and how he'd gained access. Even if he couldn't bring back the prize on this dive, he could get there with little trouble next time.

A while later—based on the view from above and the path he'd followed, he was likely at the heart of the structure—he found himself before a door that looked like nothing that had come before it. While the rest of the building showed water damage, this looked as good as new—it was obviously unnatural.

"Let's see what's inside. Doubt it'll be a boss."

He approached with caution, and it opened all on its own. Inside, the lights were on between rows of bookshelves. Kanade moved carefully inside, and found the water ended abruptly at the doorway—a clear line of demarcation, with not a drop flowing in.

"Ah, then I needn't have worried. This should be fun."

Kanade scanned the room for anything out of place, then approached a stand at the center.

Scattered across it were an incredible number of all-white puzzle pieces. This was exactly what he'd expected, so he picked one up.

If he could complete the puzzle, he'd earn his prize. It was a real stroke of luck this room wasn't underwater. He'd feared he'd

have to constantly surface and come back, but without that distraction, he could focus on completing the puzzle.

He took a breath, sat down on the chair, and began studying the pieces, memorizing the shapes of each and every one. The more he looked, the more he started finding connections.

Like Sally's evasion, this was an approach all Kanade's own, not one anyone else could imitate.

"Wonder if there's any more hints in here?"

The walls were lined with shelves that were full of books. Curious, Kanade abandoned the puzzle temporarily to flip through one of them.

"Hmm… Looks like more detailed versions of the stories in the Guild Home's basement."

Lots of setting stuff for the eighth stratum—no direct clues to dungeon locations, and nothing written in the code only he could read. But there *was* some information here; it might help them predict what sort of foes they'd encounter, and where they might find dungeons.

Flipping through was enough for Kanade to memorize the contents, and he could recall them later as needed.

Since coming here again would be significantly harder than simply committing everything to memory, he started working through all the books.

"Sadly, this doesn't lead to the next piece that easily."

In less than half an hour, he'd memorized the entire library, and was back to work on the puzzle. Only the sound of pieces slotting into place could be heard. White pieces gradually filled the inside of the frame.

"I've got the hang of this by now."

With nothing but white pieces, there was no pleasure to be taken in the picture that would eventually appear. He was getting rather bored.

Most people wouldn't be able to achieve such steady progress on a puzzle like this, but Kanade was special like that.

He really had worked out the trick to it. All it took was a prolonged period of focus, and the puzzle came together like magic.

"Whew... How's that?"

Naturally, not a piece was out of place. Kanade waited to see what would happen—and the puzzle began to glow. Like he'd hoped, a Rubik's Cube appeared above it.

"I thought so! Good."

He reached out for it, and like Sorcerer's Stacks had, it fused with Akashic Records. He checked his wand, looking for the new skill.

> **Technical Archive**
>
> Allows skills that don't require MP to be stashed as manuals on a specialized bookshelf.
> Any skills stashed this way are unavailable until the manual itself is used.

Essentially, it would let him store any skills Sorcerer's Stacks didn't. As long as he had time to prep it, he'd have access to a lot more powerful tools.

"Gotta report this one! Wonder where everyone's at?"

As he imagined them all exploring in their own ways, Kanade left the room. He wasn't overly concerned about his own reward. Not when compared to the unpredictable discoveries his guildmates would uncover. He was excited to find out what surprises they'd come back with.

Kanade got back to the Guild Home to find Maple and Sally chatting.

"Oh, Kanade! How'd it go?"

"Finished it in one," he said, filling them in on Technical Archive.

"So you can store any skills…even ones for weapons you don't use?"

"Those won't actually activate. Well…that's not quite right. I can store the manuals, and if I use them, they vanish—so it's just ineffective."

In that case, whether it could technically activate or not didn't really matter. Sally looked disappointed. To hear Kanade tell it, the Rubik's Cube and the accompanying bookshelves meshed well with the Akashic Records skill, but weren't necessarily wand-exclusive. It was possible to add them to any weapon type.

And no matter what kind of weapon a player used, getting that ability would undoubtedly increase their combat options.

"Still, no telling if you'll meet the conditions. Are you good at puzzles?"

"Uh…right, no."

Kanade hadn't exactly fought bosses for these, so Sally decided she was unlikely to pull off the same feat. Being good at fighting wouldn't get her Technical Archive. She wasn't exactly bad at puzzles, but she was definitely not someone who could make quick work of a blank puzzle. And taking full advantage of it required Akashic Records anyway, so it was definitely a mage-oriented skill.

"I could do it for you?"

"Nah, I'd wanna do it myself."

"Heh-heh, I figured."

"Did you just stumble across it?" Maple asked.

"No, it was in the hints in the basement. Not that you'd figure it out if you hadn't hit up all the libraries before."

He told them about the code, and they both looked amazed.

"Well, if I see any more codes, I'll make sure to bring back pictures."

"Yep! Okay…have we seen any before?"

"Good question. You've certainly been more places than I have, so there might have been."

"Well, let's not overlook them next time!"

"Ah-ha-ha. Wanna learn the code yourself? If they look like letters to you, you won't miss them as easily."

He promised the cipher wasn't that complicated, and they decided it was worth a try.

"Then I'll start you off easy. Even knowing a few characters will help."

"……When you say 'complicated,' do you mean by *your* standards, Kanade?"

"Augh! That would be super hard!"

"Oh yeah?" he said, smirking. Then he started teaching them what he knew.

They spent a while learning the new language, and made some progress, but eventually called it a day.

"Well?"

"I—I guess…?"

"I've learned this much."

"There's books on it on every floor in the library, so you can always reference it there if you feel like it."

Kanade had only seen real hints in this language on the current stratum, but it was always possible such hints could be found elsewhere, too.

Didn't hurt to learn the language.

"Or you could always just pop me a message if you see something likely. I'll know if it's real."

"Really? Great!"

"Then…we didn't really need to learn it ourselves?"

"But it's fun learning what you don't know."

"You've got a point."

"It was a good experience, right?"

"True… I guess I haven't done much like that."

There were plenty of games that had fake languages in them, but not many that required you to actually learn them. Especially not in the action-packed games Sally gravitated toward.

"I'm gonna take another look around town. I think towns will be pretty important on this floor."

"They might have hints like the ones in the basement!"

"Mm-hmm, and if I find any, I'll let you know. Some places I might not be able to handle solo."

"I'll be happy to help."

"Same!"

"Can't wait to see what you two find."

"Got it! I'm gonna poke around!"

Kanade shot them a grin, then headed out of the Guild Home.

Left on their own, the girls kept chatting.

"So, what's the plan? We were trying to decide where to explore next, right?"

"Given what Kanade said…I feel like going somewhere we haven't been!"

"Okay. Let's take a look at the map. Kinda…hard to just scan the horizon on this floor."

On the eighth stratum, it was just water everywhere. Since there was always a time limit, it was best to have a plan in mind before they left.

"Any leads?"

"Um…not really. Since we're still in the upgrade grind, we haven't really got much intel."

"Right…that's rough. I only just got my upgrade done!"

"But I do have one idea."

"Oh?"

"It's probably just a dungeon, but I did spot an underwater shrine."

"Ohhh! That sounds neat."

"The monsters looked pretty tough, so I figured I'd bring you along."

Sally was spinning her new dagger. She fought alongside Maple more than anyone, so this might be a good chance to practice their teamwork with her new skills.

"Those skills did seem tricky…"

"But you can just play like you always do, Maple. I'll follow your lead. Not that there's much I can do against monsters."

Monsters didn't exactly overthink things or misread situations. Maple often managed to take advantage of that, but it wasn't like things always went her way.

"All right! Let's give it a go!"

"I know how to get there, so this is the perfect excuse."

"For wha— Oh!"

Maple's eyes sparkled, and Sally led her out of the home to the water's edge, where she took a Jet Ski out of her inventory—naturally, one of Iz's creations.

It hit the water with a splash, and soon stabilized. Sally hopped on, then reached out, helping Maple clamber on behind.

"Hold on tight!"

"Okay! I can't ride these myself, so I can't wait!"

Maple had no DEX at all, so she couldn't control the Jet Ski. Sally, however, was totally fine.

"Then let's do this!"

"Ready!"

Once she was sure Maple wasn't going to fall off, Sally revved forward, gradually picking up speed.

"Whoa! It's so fast!"

"It's not easy moving quick on water. Gotta thank Iz later!"

Water spraying behind them, they headed toward the submerged shrine.

After a lengthy skiing session, Sally stopped the Jet Ski over an empty patch of water and checked her map.

"Is this it?" Maple asked.

"Yeah, we dive a bit, and there's a magic circle that'll take us somewhere that isn't underwater, so I figured it would be good."

Maple, Mai, and Yui all had extreme builds that made it impossible for them to acquire the Swimming and Diving skills at all; no matter how much they swam around the eighth stratum, they'd never boost their underwater performance beyond what the diving suits provided.

For that reason, it was hard for them to get through longer dungeons—as such, it was a relief that some dungeons weren't actually submerged.

"It's almost weird having it *not* be full of water."

"Could be like that library Kanade found, with a barrier keeping the water out. But we're underwater till we get there."

"We can make it if we hurry!"

"Exactly. Let's."

"Yeah!"

They donned their diving suits and dove in.

"You come here a lot, Sally?"

"I guess. It's a big place, and there's tons I haven't explored yet. Maple, incoming! No piercing damage!"

Sally pointed at a school of smaller fish swimming their way,

while conveying the minimal intel necessary to Maple. Those words alone told Maple what to do. Up against crowds with no piercing damage, she fared better than Sally.

"Martyr's Devotion!"

Light filled the water, and white wings unfurled behind her. The fish charged into the cylindrical column of light, surrounding them—but, protected by the skill, Sally was unharmed. Of course, so was Maple herself.

"Thanks, Maple. Not all of them are monsters, but there's still a lot."

"Whew! …Neat, never been *inside* before…"

They were actually being battered from all sides, but with Maple around, it was just like serenely swimming through a school of fish, enjoying the view.

Light from above was glittering off the fishes' scales, and they were at the heart of the school, with fish in every direction, both above and below.

"Pretty sure only you could get inside *this*, Maple. But if they can't hurt us, we could just leave them be? They are pretty."

"Yeah! I wonder if I could reach out and grab one?"

"With your stats…hard to say. Might not matter."

Maple tried snatching a few passing fish but wound up just getting her hands slapped away. They reached the bottom without her succeeding.

"Aww, no luck."

"We're pretty far down now, so…"

Even as Sally spoke, they left the school's active range, and the fish swam back up toward the surface.

"Ack! Oh no, they went away."

"There's no way I would've seen that on my own."

"Heh-heh-heh, glad to have me with you?"

"Yep. Luck was with us. But we're here for—"

"The submerged shrine!"

Sally took Maple's hand so she wouldn't fall behind and headed down toward the ruined buildings on the ocean floor. They swam through the remains of a town to what had once been a shrine, but was now more a pile of fallen columns. Fish and mollusks had made it their home, but between those columns, they spied the glow of the magic circle.

"Is that it?"

"Yep."

"You'd never spot that from the surface."

"Best to check out anything that looks even slightly unusual. If you're going hint-free, you should probably dive down a bit before you even start looking."

They might not have spotted the circle itself, but the sunken town was easy enough to spot from above. Skimming the water's surface was like flying over previous stratums; like Sally said, some things could only be found lower down.

"Well, no use treading water. Let's head on in! Gotta squeeze through that gap."

"Is that really the best approach?"

They found a gap large enough to fit through and headed for the circle in back. Since they were underwater, it was easy to move vertically, and even Maple had no trouble getting past the blockage.

"Then…on three?"

"Yeah! Ready when you are!"

"One, two…three!"

The instant they stepped on the magic circle, they were enveloped in light and taken to the shrine's interior.

When the light died down and they could see again, Maple's head started swiveling as she scoped things out.

They were at the center of an open space made of pale-blue stone. There were gaps in the walls, likely passages leading off in all directions, and stairs and canals running all across the floor. It would likely be hard to find the right path.

They took off their diving suits and began discussing their approach.

"Well? Do you know which way to go, Sally?"

"I don't, no. I did find a few hints for deeper in, but no full guide."

"Then I guess we'll just check one at a time!"

There were tons of paths to follow, and since they could also just ignore those in favor of traveling through the air, they had even more options.

This time, however, they decided not to go for a ride on Syrup or swing around on Sally's webs. It was hard enough to figure out the right route though this dungeon; taking weird shortcuts might well mean they'd skip important switches. In that case, they'd have to backtrack—so it was best to stick to the intended approach.

With that settled, they took the path straight ahead.

"Are the monsters here tough?"

"Mm-hmm, high stats, not a lot of obvious weaknesses. Oh, speak of the devil."

A blue magic circle appeared on the floor ahead of them, and a column of water shot out of it. Pushing through that water, two golems emerged—simple stone parts held together by flowing water.

"Shrine guardians?"

"Ooh, they're defending it!"

"Then let's break though. Quick Change."

Sally used a newly acquired skill to switch from her usual blue garb to her new unique series—it had a gray base, with yellow polygons generated here and there.

"I got you covered! Go ahead and try stuff out!" Maple said, raising her shield. She activated Martyr's Devotion, ready to back Sally up if anything went wrong.

"Okay, here goes."

"I'll lay down some fire! Full Deploy!"

Once Maple's weapons were ready, Sally darted forward. The golems moved to intercept, making full use of their liquid joints to flail their arms like whips.

"Whoa! They're stretchy!"

"I'm fine!"

Their range was far greater than Sally's, and to top it off she had to deal with both at once—but her feet never even paused. She just charged in, ducking under the first arm, and knocking it aside with her dagger. Then she shifted her weapon into a spear that she jammed into the ground, vaulting herself into the air, at which point she changed it back into a dagger to dodge the second arm.

"Wow!"

As Maple cheered her on, Sally landed. The second golem came in swinging a moment later—but she was ready for it.

"Hooh...!"

She had Maple's protection, so this was her chance to experiment. She switched her weapon to a greatsword and slammed the blade into the arm descending toward her, then used a great shield to deflect the other one, finally reverting it to a dagger as she advanced.

"Hahh!"

With Maple covering her, she slipped under the arm, slashing the golem in its side.

Attacks that her daggers could never have blocked were safely handled with sword and shield.

Behind the golem, Sally spun, shifting to a greatsword with a horizontal slash, then backstepping away.

She'd hit both at once, taking advantage of the sword's superior length—not something she'd ever been capable of with a dagger.

The golems staggered, and since they'd been caught in a pincer by the girls, one went after Maple, while the other turned toward Sally, attacking.

Something glowed blue at the golems' centers, then sprayed water at the girls like laser beams.

"Whoa! Oh, okay! Didn't do anything!"

Maple had been watching Sally, so she failed to respond at all; it hit her right in the torso, accomplishing nothing. She fired some lasers back, scorching the golem. Meanwhile, Sally had dodged without needing an assist from Martyr's Devotion and was soon closing the gap again.

"Maple, deploy your left arm!"

"Got it! Deploy Left Arm!"

Once Maple's skill was active, Sally ducked under the water stream and used that momentum to propel herself into a Leap overhead, swinging her left arm down at the golem below.

"Deploy Left Arm!" she shouted.

Sally's choker glowed, and her hand turned into the same giant gun barrel Maple sported.

"Commence Assault! Reality Twister!"

At her cry, the crimson laser she'd been charging swallowed up both golems beneath her.

Now a real attack, the strength of this blast was all too familiar, and it robbed the golems of the scant HP Maple's barrage had left behind. She'd seen this skill in use so often that her calculation of the damage was right on the money.

The golems were blown away without a trace. Sally landed, and the gun arm dissolved into yellow polygons, its role done.

It had all worked out—Sally breathed a sigh of relief, and Maple came running up to her.

"Sally! That was incredible!"

"I know, right? Well, first time putting that into practice."

"Yeah! You kept changing your weapon—and used them all just right!"

"I've used the different types of weapons in other games. And I helped Mai and Yui train here."

Sally shrugged it off, but it had been quite a feat. Maple still had plenty to learn about using her great shield—even with that as her only option, it took a while to learn how to fully take advantage of it.

"I'm planning on keeping this weapon's skill under wraps till we get a PvP event. I mean, a sudden change in reach would really shock people, right?"

"Yeah, I bet."

"Which means I gotta practice like this. The bigger the weapon, the more exposed you are after a swing."

Since her weapon always counted as a dagger, she couldn't acquire any of the skills that would compensate for those weaknesses. She had to accept the downsides and use them carefully. Or she'd be letting her dagger skills—which took advantage of being able to land extra hits and quick movements—go to waste.

"The Reality Twister cooldown is pretty long, so I won't get to try that out again soon. But like you saw, it makes a fake skill real for a moment."

"Mm-hmm. But why just your left hand? Not the whole kit?"

"I'm pretty fragile. Full Deploy would make it hard to move, and I'd be sunk if they fought back. Twisting myself out of the way isn't a real option."

"Oh! That makes sense."

Maple could stand perfectly still and soak everything, so that wasn't an issue for her. In Sally's case, a single counter spell slipping through would kill her instantly.

"Maybe I'll try using partial deployment more often, then."

"That would certainly help me. Hologram can only duplicate skills someone else used."

"Gotcha! Should we move on?"

They'd only just started exploring this shrine, so they resumed their journey farther in.

They moved through the shrine, listening to the sound of flowing water. In combat, Maple stuck to defending, while Sally fought up close. The new unique series had boosted her stats, but given the way the skills worked, the damage she did to monsters wasn't really that different.

"You're amazing Sally. You can use all the weapons!"

"It's just experience. But everyone's got their own style. If you're good at what you do, that's plenty."

Sally had a good grasp of her own strengths, and that had led to her current style—but it was hard to really say the same for Maple. Fortunately, this was a game where a player's own talent mattered less than the strength of the skills they'd found. Maple was more than capable in a fight with those alone.

"You've got stronger skills than me and are great when outnumbered. You're making your thing work for you."

"That's true."

"There's tons of stuff only you can do! I know you know that."

"Heh-heh! No one can beat my defense!"

"Yep. And we'll keep polishing that!"

Maple's infinite defense was the core of her fighting style. This

played into her offense, and the way she rocketed herself around by exploding her own weaponry.

No one with ordinary stats could imitate that.

"Then you go on and try stuff out, Sally! These golems don't seem to be a threat."

"You nullified their lasers, yeah."

As they chatted, they were moving through the dungeon. With Maple around, there was no danger of sudden death—and even the darkest dungeon was stress-free.

Carving their way through the golem guardians, they found their progress blocked by a broad stream. The current was pretty strong, and putting even one foot inside would result in them upside down at the bottom.

"What now, Maple? I bet there's a way to disable this somewhere."

"Oh?"

"Yeah. I can see more of this passage across it, which usually means there's a switch somewhere."

Maple looked around for any clues and saw three outcroppings on the wall. She reached out to touch them.

"……! Looks like I can press these, Sally!"

"Nice. Just…which one?"

It felt like all three would move, but that didn't mean she should just try one.

"I-is there a hint anywhere?"

"Not seeing anything like one. It's a big place, and we just took one of many passages; the clue might have been down one of the others."

"That sounds right."

"Wanna go look?"

"Sure!"

"Okay. Then we'll turn back here."

"If we search every corner, maybe we'll find a treasure chest!"

"True. I didn't really look that up… Might as well!"

Figuring it was best to explore thoroughly sometimes, they turned back.

"I guess we backtracked like this in one of the old games I played with you."

"Yeah, they like to hide chests and items in side passages, so if you think you're on the right path, it's often better to leave it till the end."

If you'd only missed items, you could progress without them, but what if you missed something good?

"I can look up a map if you want."

That depended on their goal here. If they just wanted items, she could look up the shortest route, but if they wanted to enjoy exploring, it was best to stay in the dark.

"You usually just go to the end, right?"

"Yeah. I think the only time I really looked up any items or quests was on the sixth stratum."

"Oh…thanks…"

Sally had skipped that floor. Maple had done research, trying to find something that would help Sally out. Sally was usually the one who looked stuff up, so her absence had made Maple more proactive there.

"Once I tried looking things up, I learned how fun that can be! There's so much out there—I can see why you always play that way."

"Glad to hear it. It never hurts to look stuff up if you're curious. Lots of places you'd never find out about otherwise."

"Like that flying castle! Whoever found that is amazing."

"You've got a solid history of making these discoveries yourself, Maple."

Maple's habit of winding up in the weirdest areas had led to her collection of freakish skills.

"Eh-heh-heh! It's just blind luck."

"Long as you're having fun… that's all that matters."

As they chatted, Maple and Sally arrived at a mural. Moving up close, they saw what looked like the current and the golems they'd fought.

"Is this it?"

"Probably. Those red things are probably the buttons."

The mural had several panels, showing the order in which to press the buttons if they wanted to make the stream stop.

"Then we just hit them like this?"

"Probably. Wanna go try?"

"Sure!"

Armed with new intel, they headed back to the first passage, and pressed the protrusions. There was a rumble, and the current stopped, allowing them to cross. All that was left was the hole the water had been gushing from.

"Wow! It actually worked, Sally!"

"Yep, guess we found the right one."

"Is there anything through this hole?"

"Huh? Um…wanna see?" Sally asked.

Maple stepped into the hole. "Yeah, I can fit!"

"Really? Okay then, worth a shot."

Things like this did often contain secrets, so Sally followed Maple through.

"Think we'll find anything?"

"Uh…it's not exactly guaranteed. But it happens."

Maple's eyes gleamed, already hoping for treasure. They moved farther in and heard a noise—like the ground shaking.

"Whoa! M-monsters?!"

"……! No, this is……!"

This wasn't a monster layer—it was a sluice. This noise could only be one thing.

"W-water?!"

"The flow only stopped for a moment! Ice Pillar! Right Hand: Web! Superspeed!"

Sally quickly blocked the water with a pillar, then snagged Maple with her webs and ran away like hell was on her heels.

After a quick dash, she heard the pillar break, and Sally's eyes went wide.

"Maple, prep Atrocity! No telling how much damage the water'll do!"

"G-got it!"

Between that and Indomitable Guardian, she'd have two layers of protection. Sally was rushing to the exit, but she knew Maple wouldn't make it out in time.

"Maple!"

"Atrocity! Unbreakable Shield!"

That cry alone had told Maple what to do, and she quickly activated her monster form. Sally flew out of the exit, and a furious fount of water launched Maple into the air, sending them both hurtling across the passage.

This was more terrain damage than piercing, but even with the damage-reduction skill active, it was shredding Maple's monster skin. With Martyr's Devotion active, she was also soaking Sally's damage, and that scraped the last of her skin away as they fell into the basin below.

There was a huge splash, then they surfaced beside the waterfall.

"Whew, that was close…but we're still here!"

"Urgh, sorry, Sally. I had no idea!"

"These things happen. What doesn't kill us…"

No harm in using a shortcut to get back where they'd been. They'd cleared it right the first time; no point in missing out on future fun.

"It's always worth poking around in corners that catch your interest. I'll always follow your lead. And if it goes wrong, I know you'll protect me."

Sally grinned at her, and Maple finally cheered up.

"Yeah!"

But as they got ready to move out, Maple frowned.

"……?"

"What?"

"M-my shield! It's gone! I might have dropped it!"

"Er, in the water?"

"Uh…probably?"

Maple stuck her face in the water, peering in, while Sally suggested a solution.

"If this was a boss that stole your gear, that'd be one thing, but if you just dropped it, you should be able to get it back using your inventory screen."

"Oh! R-right. Thanks, Sally!"

Maple had totally forgotten. She opened her inventory, and the black shield was soon back in her hand.

"Glad that worked."

"Yeah, totally. I saw something glowing down there, so I was about to dive in."

"Glowing…? Hmm."

That got Sally's attention, so she put her face in the water like Maple had. After all, would a black shield really glow enough to be visible at the bottom of a plunge basin?

"Sally?"

"……Maple, it's still glowing."

"……?"
"I think…there's something down there."
"Ohhh?!"
"We stumbled into this one, huh? Wanna check it out?"
"You bet! Let's go!"
"Cool. Diving suits on!"
"On it!"
An unexpected discovery got both their hopes up.

The waterfall basin was quite deep. From above, they'd noticed nothing—but once in the water, they could clearly see something glowing below.

"Straight down."

"Mm-hmm."

Like she always did, Maple threw out Martyr's Devotion, ensuring their safety. Sally held Maple's hand so they'd stay together, and swam down into the basin.

Didn't seem like there were monsters here; they soon reached the depths, where they found gaping holes leading in all directions, and a massive, gleaming, pearlescent scale.

"Is this the glowing thing?"

"Based on its location, yeah. I haven't heard about anything like this, so it may not have been discovered yet."

The base of a waterfall in the middle of the shrine. Anyone not partied with Maple would likely not have survived the fall; reaching here safely would have required someone to press the switches in the right order, and then when the passage opened, to intentionally dive into the basin instead.

Not many players had reached this location at all yet, so it made sense that things like this had gone unnoticed.

"This isn't the regular route, right?"

"Unlikely. It's an underwater shrine, but you're not supposed to need diving suits inside it."

"Let's go deeper!"

"Yeah, just watch your dive time. Who knows what lies ahead."

All the holes looked the same, so they just picked one and headed down it.

"That was a big scale."

"Whatever's waiting for us must be huge. A secret boss? Might be wandering around."

If it had dropped a scale by the entrance, it could be like the snails in the second event, and constantly swimming around these caves.

"Gotta be careful, but quick."

"You'll hit your limit before me, Maple. I'll watch your back."

Sally led the way, keeping her eyes peeled for movement. Maple kept Martyr's Devotion going and did her best to remain vigilant.

A ways down the passage, they found the remains of a crumbled building—very much in keeping with the submerged shrine theme.

"Maybe this is the *real* shrine."

"It's *actually* underwater!"

"Yeah…but pretty smashed up."

This didn't look like water had naturally eroded it so much as something giant had forced its way through.

"Those walls look sturdy; this thing might be strong."

"But not as strong as Mai and Yui!"

This unseen monster had certainly rampaged through the shrine interior; the wreckage it left behind extended to the left and the right.

"Hmm… Which way do we go?"

"It's pretty big, so there should be a clue…yup!"

Sally had been leading the way, and she paused, beckoning Maple over. She was pointing at a glowing scale—just like the one at the entrance.

"Oooh! This must be the way!"

"It's been through here, at least. Let's keep looking."

"Yeah! Doesn't seem like there's any other monsters here."

Just as Maple said, they hadn't seen any of those golems, nor any fish monsters.

The glowing scales were easy enough to find. The shrine itself was getting darker, rubble was everywhere, and nothing else was moving—it was rather sinister.

"Maple, anything below us?"

"Nope! Not even suit upgrades."

"Then we'll just have to keep moving. If anything's coming, the vibe here should shift noticeably. Just keep an eye on your oxygen."

"Okay!"

They had no idea if there'd be a place to surface. The lack of anything blocking their progress suggested that whatever waited for them was just that strong.

Endurance battles were one of Maple's classic victory strategies, but in this environment, that wasn't an option—like Sally said, haste was essential.

"I'll do quick checks of anything on the side. We're pretty far in, so I think I'll spot anything out of place."

"You know it, Sally!"

There might be hidden entrances—like the one that had led them here in the first place.

On the lookout for those, they headed toward whatever waited in the depths.

Spying no real patterns, they simply followed the trail of scales

embedded in the walls or ground. The dimly lit shrine grew darker and darker, and it was getting hard to see.

They'd been forced to put on headlamps; Sally was darting back and forth, looking for anything off the beaten path.

"Oh, another scale!"

"They're easier to find when it's this dark. It's not *too* dark to see, but definitely takes more work to avoid missing stuff."

Maple had gotten ahead of her, so Sally caught up, examining the scale in case it hid any other clues. Then she felt a vibration—like something scraping the ground.

"……Did you feel that?"

"Yep. Not your imagination!"

Something had moved down below. They weren't far from their goal.

"With visibility this low, be careful. If you're in trouble, kill Martyr's Devotion."

"Got it. You need anything, say the word!"

"Of course. I'm counting on you!"

Watching for attacks, they moved on. Though it was dark, they could tell the tunnel had ended, and they were emerging into a larger chamber.

"Wow… That's even darker!"

"……But something's here."

"Oh?!"

Maple followed Sally's gaze, looking down. There was a shadow moving around down there—its breath was causing tremors.

They braced themselves. Dim lights began appearing around the bottom of the pool, gradually illuminating the creature below.

These lights were coming from the same scales they'd found

on the way here. But these hadn't been shed—instead, the glowing scales were moving in unison.

A massive monster—part-fish, part-dragon—covered in faintly glowing scales. Its limbs had regressed, functioning more like fins, and it had several spindly growths—feelers? Tentacles? As its scales lit up the room, the creature lifted its head, the sandy bottom swirling around it.

"It's huge!"

"No telling what it'll do. Careful!"

They hefted their weapons as the boss shot upward, generating a current. It was much faster than its bulk suggested. Sally kicked hard, jolting herself into action.

"Superspeed!"

"C-cover Move!"

Warping after Sally's burst of speed let Maple avoid a direct hit, but the current in the boss's wake swept them both up.

While they swapped positions, they saw the boss's tail fin move as it turned to face them.

"Faster than I thought! Maple, can you dodge that?"

"I don't think so!"

At Maple's speed, she wouldn't be able to swim out of the way. Unless Sally stayed close, Maple wasn't avoiding this boss.

"I'm gonna let it hit me once! Nothing that charges has ever been piercing."

"……Okay. Then let's split up. You draw it to you, and I'll move around, attacking."

"Right!"

If the charge did do piercing damage, they'd have to reverse their roles. Certain it was charging again, Sally swam off, avoiding the charge and moving into its blind spot.

"Taunt!"

Maple braced her shield, letting the boss hit it. But she was underwater—things didn't work the same as they did on land.

"Whoaaa!"

Devour hit the boss's head, doing considerable damage—but the charge itself was unabated, and Maple was sent rocketing away through the water.

She hit the bottom, and sediment filled the water above the impact.

"Gotta do what we can. Water Cowl!"

Sally was a bit worried about Maple, but Indomitable Guardian hadn't been used up yet, so she knew Maple'd survived that hit. In which case, it was her job to take advantage of the opening Maple had given her. Wielding the dual daggers from her blue gear, Sally swam along the boss's lengthy back, slashing like crazy. Each hit carried added damage, so even with the lower stats from this loadout, she actually did more damage wearing it.

"At that size, you can't exactly turn quick!"

It did turn and try to shake her off, but by then she'd backed off, swimming around so it couldn't get at her.

"Full Deploy! Commence Assault!"

From the murk at the bottom, a barrage of bullets and lasers emerged.

"Sally! I'm okay!"

Maple's signature defense had handled the massive boss's charge just fine, and her voice rang out above the gunfire.

"Good! That's a relief! I'm gonna focus on offense!"

The boss's attacks really took advantage of its size; against an ordinary party, it was too big to avoid, and players would be slammed hard for massive damage—but if you overturned that premise, it was no big deal.

Sally could dodge it. Maple could soak it.

Charges, tail sweeps, always moving, always attacking—and none of it doing any harm. Standard attacks in a set pattern just could not make this duo crumble.

It had high stats to compensate, but not high enough to deal with Maple; and those stats meant nothing if it couldn't even hit Sally.

The giant sleeping at the bottom had seemed threatening, but in action, it failed to live up to expectations. They were steadily chipping away at its HP.

"Saturating Chaos!"

The boss was coming at her for the umpteenth time, maw gaping wide, so Maple threw a summons of her own right at it, ripping away a chunk of its health pool, and stopped the charge dead.

"I'm not done yet!" she cried, firing her guns. Sally seized the opportunity to get a few hits in herself, but rather than fight back, the boss shook them off, rocketing upward faster than even Sally could follow.

"Huh? It left?"

"No, it's not running!"

At the top of the room, the boss turned toward them, upside down. Its feelers followed suit, reaching out in front of it.

Far out of their range, the glow on the scales began to fade, starting at the tail—and the boss's body dissolved into the darkness.

But the glow wasn't gone; it was just concentrating itself at the tips of the boss's feelers.

At this point, Maple had seen enough similar animations to guess what would happen.

"It's gonna fire something?!"

"It will! Brace yourself!"

"Heavy Body! Piece Guard!"

Maple threw out skills and raised her shield. As she hit her defensive stance, a column of light slammed down on them.

"I'm good! Stay behind me!"

"Mm-hmm, this is all you."

As Sally took shelter, light surrounded them. It was so bright that for a moment they couldn't see anything else. Maple's shield swallowed it—but before it could get everything, the light burst, scattering in all directions.

"Huh?"

Maple's eyes followed the light—and saw black scales studding the floor and walls, absorbing the light.

"That…doesn't look good."

Sally's hunch was right. When the light from the boss stopped, these scales became generators and reflectors, sending smaller beams in every direction.

"Sally."

"Yeah. Better to keep it up. I'll do my best to dodge 'em, but…"

That settled the Martyr's Devotion question—the bouncing lights were now too frequent for them to ignore.

The boss's own scales had not regained their luster—it likely couldn't fire its main beam attack again without a lengthy recharge.

"Just watch out for its usual attacks! Those'll send you flying."

"Right! Gonna go on the offense!"

Maple put her back to the wall. This way, if it tackled her, she would just be pinned in place—this stabilized the range of Martyr's Devotion, and made it easier for Sally to plan her attacks from within the safety of its boundaries. This was a position Maple could only assume because she took no damage.

Sally swam upward, closing in on the boss—but naturally, the beams of lights bouncing between the scales flew her way.

"Good practice. I've gotta…dodge this much!"

Being underwater changed everything, but Sally made it seem like the terrain didn't matter. She used quick breaks and sudden surges to thread her way through the hail of projectiles, toward the boss.

Slipping through volleys was just a core survival skill for Sally. This was how she fought enemies designed to handle her build; she'd *had* to learn how, or she'd never even get in the ring.

"Triple Slash!"

The skill effects from her attack gleamed in the darkened water.

With its glow gone, the boss blended in with the darkness and was hard to make out—but Sally's motions were every bit as precise.

"Gotta make this stuff feel easy…!"

Dodging more beams and moving back as the boss writhed to bat her away, she strove for even better performance.

Sally had her own goals, but those didn't really mean this boss had a chance of hitting her.

She had room for improvement, but even a flawed performance was enough to make her untouchable.

"Maple, it's moving!"

"Got it! Lure of the Deep!"

Swelling up from inside the suit, leaking a murk even darker than the dark water—Maple turned her arm into tentacles.

If she didn't even need her shield to avoid taking damage, then she could devote all her energy to gobbling up her enemy with her all-consuming arm.

The five tentacles coiled around the charging boss's head, crushing it. Power didn't matter—they devoured all they touched. With the boss unable to resist, there was a massive spray of damage sparks.

"Whoa! It's not stopping!"

Maple had taken a chunk out of its head but had not slowed its momentum. The boss's bulk slammed Maple up against the wall, trying to crush her.

That did flatten all the weapons she had, but since it literally couldn't be any closer to her, this opened up all sorts of other attack options.

"Predators! Saturating Chaos!"

Three monsters tore into the boss, and the tentacles squeezed again. By the time it pulled away, she'd seriously diminished its HP.

"No poison, so...Deploy Artillery!"

Poison was off-limits because it would hurt everything in the water except Maple herself. Instead, she generated a bunch of guns over her shoulders, and fired them all at the boss's retreating back.

"Sally! It's headed your way!"

"On it!"

Giving up on Maple, the boss targeted Sally, but the futility of that was already a forgone conclusion. Not one of the innumerable laser beams had hit her while the boss was going after Maple.

This duo's defenses had no clear time limits. One might have been due to pure talent, and the other always-active in-game skills, but if attacks didn't hit or didn't hurt, it didn't matter how long they had to fight.

"Cyclone Cutter! Quintuple Slash!"

Neither unique skills nor finishing moves—these were just moves earned from going down basic skill trees. But the toll they exacted on the boss was significant. If you were the only one doing damage, you needed nothing more.

And if that need *did* arise, Sally could momentarily borrow Maple's power.

"Quick Change! Deploy Artillery!"

Yellow polygons gathered on Sally's back, sprouting several cannons—which fired exactly like Maple's.

"Reality Twister!"

Delivered at point-blank range, the attack pierced the boss and came out the other side. Mingled with a spray of damage sparks, the weapon itself collapsed in a flash of yellow light.

"If I can't keep firing, it doesn't hit as hard as the real version, hmm? Maple, finish it!"

"Right!"

Seeing a barrage of lasers headed her way, Sally shifted her weapon to a shield, protecting herself as she backed away from the boss.

There was an explosion below, and Maple took Sally's place, rocketing in with lasers flying everywhere.

She planted herself right on the boss's kisser, blasting it from even closer than Sally had been.

"How's that?!"

Red beams went right through the boss—for a second, it glowed brighter than ever before, then burst into a shower of light.

"Whew… Nice work."

"Same to you, Sally! Seriously, you could have stayed inside Martyr's Devotion."

"True. But if I don't make a habit of dodging, I'll get rusty. And this one mostly kept its distance."

Since they had limited time down here, they'd had to beat it quickly.

"Everything's so fast! It's hard to catch them underwater."

"I'd have ducked into range if I was in real trouble."

"Yup! Well, that's what it's for!"

"Thanks. But what now? The scales are even brighter, but…"

They'd lit up when the boss died, turning a beautiful shade of white and making it much easier to see in here.

The girls looked around for anything worth taking back with them—and spotted a distinctive pile of scales.

"Guess we can take these with us?"

"Yeah! Wow! They're big!"

"Matches the boss."

"I could have made my white shield way faster with scales this size."

"Right, you were farming scales for that. Without the fishing skill..."

"I couldn't catch much, but had to fish anyway...but now I've got this, and can tag along with you!"

Maple pointed at her diving suit.

"Heh-heh, all hail the diving suit. I never thought I'd adventure underwater with you, Maple. If you need them, go ahead. If you show them to Iz, she might be able to upgrade your white gear."

"You're sure?"

"I just found a whole new set."

Since Sally only owned unique gear, she couldn't upgrade it. That made sense, so Maple put the scales in her inventory. As the heap of scales vanished, she spotted something else glowing beneath them.

"There's more?"

"Looks like. Pack up those scales and we'll see."

Sally started helping, and once the scales were gone, the glow beneath them became clear.

It was a clump of light. No corporeal form—their hands passed right through it. But it did count as an item, and they could move it to their inventories.

"What is it?"

"Something rare? There's only one."

"Maybe! It's yours, Sally!"

"Er, mine? I'm good, you take it."

"Hng…but that means I'm taking everything. I already took the scales."

If Maple took this, too, all Sally would get out of this was a bit of XP. That hardly seemed fair.

"……I really don't need anything. Uh, well, let's at least see what it is. If it's equippable, I'll reconsider."

"Got it! Let's see."

Maple put the clump of light in her inventory, and checked its name.

"Um…Light from Heaven. Weird thing to find underwater."

"……Curious. What's the description say?"

"Uh…this was in the sky once, yada yada. Wanna read it?"

"Sure."

Sally took a look, and it sure was some flavor text. Didn't seem equippable or like it directly led to a quest.

"Didn't you find something else weird a while back?"

"Um…oh, Lost Legacy?"

"Yeah. They might both have uses down the line. They're both rare drops from hidden bosses, right?"

"Oh-ho. Maybe."

"It might be on the eighth stratum somewhere. We'll have to look."

"Yup, yup."

"Check it out, there's an exit circle. Shall we? Before you drown."

"Wah! We'd better book it!"

Sally led her to the magic circle, and they left the submerged shrine.

As it lifted them to the surface, Maple frowned like she was forgetting something.

"Oh! Sally, the rare item…!"

"You noticed? Yeah, hang onto it for now."

"Argh," Maple sulked.

Sally had smoothly let the Light from Heaven stay in Maple's inventory.

"Sorry. What say we look for the place it goes together? That said, I don't have your luck or instincts, so I bet you're the one who finds it."

"I wouldn't say that! But of course, I don't mind. Just…"

It felt like Sally was always helping her. Seeing this coming, Sally pointed out the rational upsides for her.

"Maple, you're always finding weird skills, right?"

"Well…it happens."

"So if I go there with you, I might learn a few things about how you do it. That could be huge. This game's got loads of powerful skills. I mean, I've got new skills—but you can't use them. So it's your turn."

Sally had picked up Hologram and Reality Twister. Now that she had those, the best thing for their overall performance would be for Maple to pick up something new, too. Seeing firsthand how effective these new skills had been, Maple had to concede the point.

"Fair…I guess. But I feel like you spun a web of words around me."

"Ah-ha-ha, did I? Really, don't worry about it. I'm pleased with what I got. But if it bugs you, I'll take the next thing."

"Okay! That works!"

"Then let's shake on it."

Wondering how to use the two mystery items, they headed back to the Guild Home.

At a later date, Maple and Sally were chatting in the Guild Home. They'd agreed to search for a place to use these weird items, but the items themselves were their sole hint.

They had them spread out on the table and were looking them over when the other guild members got back.

"Oh, you're both here… What are those?"

Chrome saw the items on the table first.

"Things Maple found but can't figure out how to use."

"Maple's discoveries…and you're clueless, otherwise?"

"Exactly! I can't dive much, or explore for long…so I haven't found anything."

"What are they called?"

"Um, this box is Lost Legacy. And the glowy thing is Light from Heaven."

"Those are some names. Once you do find a use, it'll likely lead to some hidden event."

"Any ideas, Mai?"

"Um… I've never seen anything that matches those names."

"So the names themselves are clues. I've seen veiled references on stone slabs that might be related."

"Really?!"

"Then these were in that made-up language? Yeah, if you know about these items, texts in that language might read different."

"Mm-hmm, but don't get excited yet. I bet we'll need our suits fully upgraded before we can take advantage of them."

Maple Tree were all gathering upgrade parts, but it would still be a while before they were done.

"Oh, okay. But tell us about anything that might be a hint!"

"Will do. I've got one about the light—it says 'from heaven,' but before everything sank, what counted as the sky was much lower down, right?"

"Oh, is that why we found it underwater?"

"Possibly. So it must be somewhere high enough they'd have called it 'heaven.'"

"That's what I thought, yeah. And Lost Legacy is likely related to the machines we see around town."

"Could be, yeah," Chrome said. "There aren't as many as there were on the third stratum, but there are quite a few below the water."

The screen and light guns in the dungeon Sally had cleared were certainly good examples, but even outside that area, they frequently saw broken machines stuck on boulders or buildings.

"Yes, and that gives me more items to craft."

"Heh-heh, then somewhere with lots of machines, too?"

"Have you seen anything? Probably need to upgrade the suits, yeah."

"The slabs talk about an ancient civilization, so probably pretty deep."

"If that's a lost civilization, it ties into the item name. You could be onto something."

"We'll have to keep an eye out as we gather parts!"

"I-I'll do my best!"

"Thanks, everyone. Let's come back with something amazing!"

"You always do, Maple. Sometimes it's scary."

"I know, right?"

"You can say that again."

Maple had found far too many things that counted as "amazing." Everyone was glad to see their guild get stronger, but everything she found was completely crazy.

Chrome, Iz, and Kasumi were shaking their heads, but with a viable-sounding hint, Maple herself was just motivated.

CHAPTER 4

Defense Build and the Sunken Ship

A while after that, all eight members of Maple Tree had gained access to the entirety of the eighth stratum. Which meant only one task was on their minds.

"Sally! We can finally go wherever we want!"

"Yep. Let's go see if we can find anything."

They were looking for the place these two mystery items led to.

Naturally, they'd kept an eye out for hints during the upgrade grind, but had come up empty. Possibly it was just so well hidden they'd missed it, but best to start by scouring uncharted waters.

They knew those had far more secrets in them.

"Anytime, Sally!"

"In that case, why not now? You've got what Iz made?"

"Yup! Loads of stuff that makes it easier to catch a breath."

"Then let's head out. Ultimately, we'll have to hit up all the spots, so no reason to put it off."

Outside the Guild Home, Sally prepped her Jet Ski, and sat Maple behind her.

"Hold on tight!"

"I am!"

Sally opened the throttle all the way, and they shot off across the water's surface.

"Where are we starting?"

"The biggest of the newly opened areas. Isolated locations are harder to explore in rapid succession, so I figured we'd leave them till later."

"Makes sense."

"And this location is pretty elevated, so it's at or near the top of our candidate list."

"Wow! What if we stumble across it first thing?"

"That would make having done our homework pay off."

For a while, the Jet Ski raced on. Checking her map, Sally brought it to a halt.

"Under here?"

"No, a bit farther off but…well, you'll see."

Maple looked puzzled but put her diving suit on. The girls dove in. Like in the rest of the stratum, they found themselves in a vast expanse of water. Below them, there was a mountain range surrounded by a violent current—like a storm raging under the surface.

The current had visual effects added to it, making it easy to spot, but not so they could plan a route through it—more a warning that if you tried to approach, you'd get swept to your doom.

"I bet you could survive it, but…if you get stuck inside, I can't pull you out, so better not try."

"Uh, all right. I'll be careful."

She'd had bad luck with currents before, so Maple vowed to keep her distance.

"So we can't go that way?"

"Actually, we have to."

"Huh?!"

Sally had just finished explaining the threats and convincing Maple to stay clear.

"There *is* a way. We just have to examine the currents carefully."

"Okay. You know the way, Sally?"

"I didn't find anything on what lies inside, but I did find the location of the entrance."

"Wow! Good work."

They swam to the ocean floor nearby, and then down the slope toward the base of the mountain. The powerful current didn't reach all the way to what had once been ground level, and presented no barriers to access.

"Given the size of the mountain range, I'm sure there's several entrances…but this is one we know about."

Before them lay a cave leading into the mountain itself. They didn't know if there were sources of breathable air within, but from the outside it appeared entirely flooded.

"If it seems dangerous, we can always evac. Be careful not to let yourself drown."

"Got it! Let's hope it isn't too long."

Together, they plunged into the flooded cave. The lighting within was adjusted, keeping it from getting too dark to see in.

They were unsure if this was a dungeon—or if it had monsters—so for now they headed onward without deploying Martyr's Devotion.

"Hmm? Was that…?"

"Monsters. Hard to make out!"

Bobbing through the water ahead were three liquidy, slime-like creatures. They would've been hard to spot at all if they weren't slightly darker than the water around them, making their outlines visible.

"Whoever attacks first, wins!"

Maple deployed her weapons and unleashed a barrage in their general direction.

This would normally have made short work of the average trash mob—but not this time.

The approaching projectiles put the slimes in combat mode, and they stretched their bodies out thin and broad, catching all of Maple's shots.

The rounds failed to penetrate the slimes—instead, they stretched the slimes to their limits, and then, as their bodies snapped back, the projectiles were sent flying back where they'd come from.

"C-cover!"

Maple hid her shield behind her, moving in front of Sally and soaking the rebounded bullets.

She wasn't about to take damage from her own attacks, but if any happened to hit Sally, they'd spell instant death.

"Guess it's gotta be magic."

"Um...then..."

"Let's not use poison, mmkay?"

"Riiiight."

Maple's main offensive tactics involved Machine God, Saturating Chaos, and Hydra. Only Hydra counted as magic. But if she dropped poison in the water, it would hurt everything in the vicinity—they'd confirmed that ages ago.

Devour would likely swallow these up, but there was no use wasting it on ordinary enemies.

"I've got items that'll make my weapons hurt them, but they don't affect Machine God, so...Sally!"

"Yup, this is all me."

There was no need for Maple to find some clever solution to this. This sort of thing was exactly why Sally had obtained a broad range of core skills.

"I'll match your pace!" Maple said. "Can't exactly hang back shooting this time."

"Okay, then do your thing."

Sally shot forward toward the slimes, and Maple caught up with Cover Move, ready for anything.

"Cyclone Cutter!"

Winds swirled on Sally's palm, growing in strength—then shot toward the slimes, swallowing them up.

This time they could not return the attack, and it did considerable damage to their gelatinous bodies.

"More fragile than expected… Is the bounce back their one trick?"

Sally's magic wasn't buffed much, and was a little underpowered by eighth-stratum standards, but given how much HP they'd lost, these slimes must have been given pretty low stats to compensate for them reflecting some attacks.

Still, it seemed that trick wasn't their sole means of attacking. The three slimes joined forces and summoned a magic circle, which fired a huge clump of water.

"Cover!"

Maple figured this wasn't piercing, and stepped in front of it. It burst on contact, generating a shock wave.

But Maple wasn't about to worry about a mere shock wave; she handled it with no problem, keeping Devour in reserve, and waited for Sally's next move.

"How's this?"

While Maple was soaking the attack, Sally had popped open her inventory and grabbed an item from it. She cracked the crystal in her hand, and it made lightning crackle on her weapons—with Water Cowl adding a water strike to her blows, she lunged in again.

"Triple Slash!"

Unlike her magic, her weapon DPS had kept pace with the game—and the added lightning effect scorched the slimes, with the water chaser claiming the last of their HP.

"Nice! Good-bye."

"Easier than I thought. The bounce back spooked me…"

"If they show up with other monsters, look out. Looks like careful item use will make weapon damage viable, so if they're on their own, we don't need to sweat it."

"Then let's move on!"

"Yeah. Don't wanna dillydally."

"There's even slimes in the water! You'd think they'd dissolve."

"True! Yeah, you don't usually see them in water levels."

Such slimes mostly bounced around up on land, not having the most aquatically advantageous forms. It had seemed like they'd mostly just drift on the currents.

"They might use their water magic if they need to move around quickly. We've seen creatures with tricks like that before…"

"Like how I use Machine God to fly around!"

"I…guess? It's in the same ballpark."

The visuals were rather different, as was the potential for collateral damage. But Sally decided to pay that no attention.

As they moved on, several types of monsters came at them—not just the slimes. Birds, beasts—all sorts of things that didn't exactly belong underwater. To allow them to function down here, they were all encased in a bluish gel—kind of like what the slimes were made out of.

"Even this floor has your typical monsters!"

"I feel like that's not quite accurate, but sure…here they are, underwater for some reason."

They were floating about casting water spells, but didn't exactly swim around as fast as fish could. Their abilities were all just like they were on land, which felt really wrong.

"Their sluggishness does help us."

"Even I have time to react!"

"See?"

If Maple could match their speed, then Sally was far, far faster. She'd been moving quicker than most eighth-stratum foes to begin with.

For that reason, they made steady progress without too much effort. The water spells were big, powerful AOEs, but with Maple around that did nothing; and all the monsters were fragile enough that Sally was strong enough to take them out on her own.

"Glad I didn't try this solo," Maple said. "I couldn't have beat anything here!"

"Well, traditionally tanks do their best work paired with a DPS. They often struggle a bit on their own."

"Heh-heh-heh! My attacks aren't too shabby, then!"

"You certainly make the most of them."

Slinging poison around, summoning monsters, riddling them with artillery—none of these were traditional tank moves.

Naturally, from a party standpoint, it was great that she could do damage, but even without that, there were plenty of ways for her to contribute.

"Farther in, we might find other kinds of monsters, and then you'll get a turn."

"Okay! I've got tons of ammo left!"

"Glad to hear it."

Unlike Maple, Sally's build wasn't based around moves with use limits; even after a lengthy exploration, their resources weren't substantially diminished.

If the boss was your standard corporeal presence, then all the skills Maple had in reserve would get their chance to shine.

After traveling through the cave a while, they reached a large chamber with several passages leading out of it. Gingerly, they stepped inside—but no miniboss spawned. It was just your standard-issue fork in the road. Feeling like this cave was far from over, Sally checked in with Maple.

"How's your air?"

"Fine! ......?"

"Maple?"

Feeling something off, Maple was patting the chest of her diving suit.

"What's wrong? Your oxygen...should be good, by the numbers."

"Does it feel kinda warm around here?"

"......Hmm. Well, doesn't seem like a status effect."

Sally gave it some thought, then an idea hit her.

"If it doesn't do damage or debuff you, and there's no monsters around, maybe it's a hint. I can't feel it myself, so maybe it's reacting to a skill or item you have."

"Whoa! Maybe!"

"Just...I can't tell if that's good or bad."

"......?"

"It could be a warning, saying there's a really tough monster up ahead. Or it could be leading us to a really good item."

Assuming it was a sign, there was no telling if it was safe to follow.

All they really knew was that something unprecedented was happening to Maple.

"What's your gut tell you, Maple?"

"Um...well, like you said, it feels like a hint. If it's stronger near one passage, let's go that way."

"Even if it leads to a crazy boss?"

"I'm with you, Sally. We'll trounce it."

Maple's smile was so dazzling it caught Sally off guard. She blinked and looked amused—then confident.

"True. With you on my side, we've got this."

"And…this way doesn't feel wrong. I mean, that could just be my imagination, but…"

"Hmm. Well, your hunches never lead us astray."

In that case, they'd better swim where the signal led them. But first, they had to figure out which passage to take.

"Let's move to each in turn. Maybe you'll notice something."

"Got it!"

Sally helped her over to the first, but Maple shook her head.

"Feels the same!"

"Next."

They took a quick dip into the mouth of each branch, and eventually one of them made Maple stop and cock her head.

"What?"

"Um…it felt warmer for like, a second?"

"Really?"

"Hard to tell."

"Then let's give it a second shot. Move along one, then come back."

"Okay! That might help."

Maple moved to the next passage, then came back, concentrating.

"Well?"

"Definitely felt it!"

"Cool. Then this must be the one."

Even the slightest difference suggested this was the right passage.

From now on, they'd have to repeat this trick at every fork.

* * *

Relying entirely on what Maple was feeling, they moved on to the next fork in the road. But before Maple could try to figure out the right path, there was a flash, and sparks flew—something electric was crackling in the center of the room.

"……!"

"Sally, something's spawning!"

"Brace yourself!"

Maple raised her shield and artillery pieces, and Sally gripped her daggers tightly, ready to attack at any time. The noise and light died down, and something was hovering in the water.

They watched closely. It looked like a stone cube. Lines ran across it, and it split into sections, a blue core gleaming from within.

An HP bar appeared overhead, and it started spinning—ready for combat.

"A bit like those golems?"

"The ones from before?"

"Yeah, it's made from the same things."

Not only was it also stone, but the coloring and general vibe were a lot like the guardians of the submerged shrine. In which case, their destination was all the more likely to be this way.

"Maybe we got lucky."

"Oh? Great! Then let's go for it!"

"Yeah, it's clearly protecting something."

This was proven by the lights it sent flying. These covered the exits in stone. Then an array of magic circles appeared around it.

"I'm ready!"

"Thanks!"

Ready to use Martyr's Devotion, they waited to see what it would do. As the circles glowed, their bodies drifted to the left.

"It's not an attack...no damage!"

"But this is...whoa!"

Rather than throwing water projectiles at them, it was transforming the entire room—a large-scale change. The circles were generating a current in the room, matching the boss's own rotation and dragging everything along with it.

"Commence Assault! Argh, I can't aim!"

Maple was trying to fire her guns, but since the effectiveness of this was reliant on her defense, she'd never really had to learn to aim while in motion and wasn't doing much damage.

"Glad it isn't one of those bosses where only the core takes damage! I'll attack, too, so just do what damage you can, Maple."

"Got it! I'm gonna catch up here!"

Since all the monsters had had water bodies, Maple was just glad to fight something she could hurt. She had plenty of ammo left, and seized her chance.

"A current like this...!"

Sally didn't try to fight it. She sped up, tightening the circle and closing in. The boss responded, generating water spears, but not before Sally got there.

"Triple Slash!"

She was only in range for an instant but did the most damage she could—a skill that left six deep gouges in the boss before the current swept her away.

"Frankly, this only helps me move faster!"

"Wow, Sally! Okay, let me..."

Taking careful aim was not Maple's strong suit. Instead, she summoned the largest gun she could, aiming at the center.

But before she could fire a laser beam, the water spears the boss had generated for Sally came in on the current.

These seemed designed to home in on anyone in the same water flow; not an issue for Sally, but Maple wasn't fast enough to escape them.

"Whoa! Hang on!"

"Don't worry, I gotcha!"

Sally moved in quick, positioned herself against the current so she stopped next to Maple, and raised her weapons to block the spears.

"Hoh...!"

Daggers darted through the water, gleaming blue, knocking every spear bound for Maple off-course.

Maple herself would likely be fine, but attacks often broke her weapons, so this sort of thing was essential.

"Thanks, Sally! Okay! Commence Assault!"

With a gun this big, she didn't need to aim—even if she was bit off-center, it would do solid damage. A massive red laser beam crossed the room, ignoring the current. It scorched the object in the center and passed through it, exploding on the far wall.

"Urgh, a little off-center."

"Good enough! Keep firing. I'll stay here and block."

"Okay!"

This was a good use of Maple's weapons, so Sally decided to defend her instead.

Their foe was desperate to smash her guns, but it was a tall order to get through Sally's parries. She wasn't just using her daggers—she was also using defensive spells like Water Wall, allowing her to block attacks from multiple directions at once.

"Okay...aiming..."

"Don't worry about me."

"Commence Assault!"

The result of all this—until her constant laser shots pulverized the boss, none of Maple's weapons took damage.

When the cube vanished, the current slowed to a stop, and the waters were peaceful once more.

"It wasn't that tough."

"It might have been tough for regular parties…but yeah, not especially challenging for us."

"Since you kept me safe, my weapons are still good! And I've got Devour!"

Sally was doing great work keeping Maple's skills in stock. With her defense, Maple could keep the lasers going constantly, and if they didn't break, she could minimize the number of weapons she'd have to make.

"Then let's go deeper. Your lead, Maple."

"Aye, aye!"

Following the signal, they swam on. There was a clear difference in the types of monsters they now faced. No longer were they up against monsters made of water; now most creatures were golems made of stone or metal.

These moved with surprising agility even underwater, attacking both physically and magically—but since they *didn't* reflect attacks, Maple actually found them much easier to handle.

"Commence Assault!"

"They sure can't stand up to *all* your bullets."

"There's no current here! I just have to shoot straight!"

She wasn't holding back on deployment, and her fusillade had just vaporized another golem.

Since these projectiles did a fixed amount of damage, and the monsters got stronger with each passing floor, the skill was gradually growing less effective—but there were still precious few foes that could survive charging directly at her guns.

These monsters weren't exactly weak, but they also didn't pose a real threat to this duo. The two of them could tackle everything directly, without resorting to schemes.

"Cool! We've got this!"

"……For a normal party, just being underwater would make a difference, and dealing with AOE attacks would make that even harder. But against you? Also, if these are coming from the shrine, that might well have been the main boss. Bosses aren't always at the end."

"Oh-ho."

They were going higher and higher in the mountain. Since they were deep inside, it was hard to tell just how high they had gone, but they could tell they were gradually ascending.

Leaving no foes unvanquished, Maple and Sally reached the top of the mountain and gazed out at the mountain range around them.

From the outside, the effect-laden current had made it hard to see much at all, but from within, things were rather unremarkable. The "peak" was broad and flat, as if it had been pounded down from above.

"Doesn't really feel like a peak, huh? We can't exactly go directly from here to anywhere else, so how's your signal— Maple?!"

Sally had turned to find Maple's chest lit up, which was alarming.

"I'm okay! It's just a light."

"Then the signal's getting stronger? There must be something here. Should we walk around a bit and see?"

"Sure!"

Maple began scouring the peak, trying not to miss a thing.

Sally tagged along behind, ready to yank her out of harm's way if anything happened. There were no signs of anything hostile, so she wasn't expecting trouble—but then Maple vanished right before her very eyes.

"Hah……?!"

No transport circle, no monsters, no terrain in which an ambush could lurk. Sally dashed forward to examine the ground Maple had been standing on, and screeched to a halt as something emerged from thin air right in front of her. She staggered backward—and realized who it was.

"M-Maple?!"

"Oh! Sally! Were you all right?"

"Er, yeah. It was real fast—and no sign of monsters emerging. But…what's going on here?"

Before Sally's eyes, Maple's head floated in the air. Technically, only the front half of it—like a mask hanging on a wall. It was downright unnerving.

"Can you come over? Give me your hand…here!"

This time an arm joined the disembodied face. Didn't seem like this was another fake Maple. And Sally trusted Maple not to take her somewhere dangerous without warning her first—so she decided it was safe to take that hand.

"Okay, holding tight."

"Then away we go!"

At Maple's urging, she took a step forward—and everything below her knee vanished, as if passing through an invisible wall. She took no damage and could clearly feel solid ground beneath the unseen foot.

Sally kept walking, moving through the invisible wall, and

found blinding light pouring down from above. The light levels were so different from on the underwater peak that she had to squint until her eyes adjusted.

"Wow…"

"Crazy, right?"

Before them lay a landscape that looked like the surface—the one thing this stratum didn't offer. The ground was covered in flowers and grass, animals were running around, and birds sang here. This place alone was not underwater—when they looked up, nothing impeded their view of the sky.

The game didn't treat this place as underwater—Maple had already removed her diving suit, so Sally did the same.

"This area is totally cut off, then. Didn't feel like we were transported in, though."

"I think the space behind you connects to the outside!"

Given how Maple had been able to lean through it, this made sense.

The animals here didn't seem hostile—they'd spotted the girls, but weren't attacking.

"Well, that aside…one thing really stands out here."

"Yup, I know! So weird-looking!"

The landscape and creatures were standard-issue for other floors, but one thing stood out like a sore thumb.

Though it was rotting away, they could still make out the shape of it—a giant wooden ship. There was a huge gouge in the side of it; plants had taken over, and animals were living within. It looked like they could explore the interior, either by entering through that gaping hole or flying up to the deck above.

"Is the light getting brighter?"

"Maybe too bright."

The signal strength certainly suggested they were getting close, and the whole vibe of this location was a dead giveaway.

"No way we're leaving without exploring that. Let's go!"

"You betcha!"

They had plenty of use-limited skills remaining. They'd wasted few resources. It would take something virtually unprecedented to take them down, so neither hesitated to continue their search.

"Where do we start?"

"Maybe we should take a proper entrance. I feel like that hole isn't one."

"Then up we go. I could web us there, but it's pretty high. Wanna handle this?"

"Sure! Syrup, Awaken!"

Maple called out her pet and made it go giant.

With no monsters around, they could fly up without worries. From Syrup's back, they had a clear view of the deck and could be sure no monsters were waiting for them—instead, they saw animals sleeping peacefully on a bed of flowers.

"Looks safe to land."

"Then let's go!"

Maple lowered them down to deck level, and once on the ship, she put Syrup back in her ring.

"Let's head in!"

"Whoo!"

They peered down the stairs leading below the deck. The interior was every bit as overgrown as the deck itself; there was no trace remaining of furnishings.

"Doesn't look like there's monsters inside…but I'll keep an eye out."

"Thanks! Wonder what we'll find?"

"It'll likely be all the way in. Somewhere not linked to other rooms or passages."

"I'll find it!"

"Mm-hmm, counting on you."

This ship was huge, but only parts of it were accessible; if Maple followed the signal, they wouldn't get lost.

In due time, they saw their destination.

A light pulsed within it, resonating with the light on Maple's chest—it was a relief on the wall, still intact despite the collapse around it.

"Doesn't...look like a boss."

"Should we approach?"

"Sure. Not sensing any enemies."

Sally kept watch while Maple approached the relief, ready for anything. The moment she touched it, the light on her chest grew extra bright, lighting up the interior.

Then there was a tremor that rocked the whole ship.

The mountain wasn't shaking—the ship itself was trying to move, propelled by some unknown power.

"Whoa?!"

"It's moving...?!"

The light was so bright they couldn't even see each other. Each did their best to remain upright—and eventually the light and rocking died down.

"I-is it over?"

"......Maybe it's no longer capable of moving. I mean, from the outside, it looked totally wrecked."

"True...."

If they could take this ship home with them, it would have been quite a prize, but that seemingly wasn't an option.

"Right! Maple, anything feel different? That was a lot of rocking, and I can't hear a system voice meant for you."

She was asking if Maple's items or skills had changed at all, so Maple double-checked.

"Um, Light from Heaven is gone, and I got…one new skill!"

"I thought so. What's it like? Can I see?"

Naturally, she meant only if it was safe to use here. But as the name of the item that had led them here implied, it wasn't especially dangerous; Maple read the description, and tried it right away.

"Glow of Deliverance!"

At her cry, there was another powerful burst of light. A halo appeared over Maple's head—Sally was used to that, but this halo was much spikier. Maple's hair turned gold, her eyes blue, and four white wings unfurled on her back as the ground around her lit up. A more dramatic change than Sally had anticipated, but she soon recovered and moved closer to inspect it.

"A lot like Martyr's Devotion… Is it an evolved version?"

"Nope, totally different! Watch… Martyr's Devotion!"

Maple's next skill added two more white wings, and a second, rounder halo within the spiky one.

"What's it do?"

"Um…increases resistance to status effects for allies in range, decreases the damage taken, and applies a heal over time!"

"Like a moving Heaven's Throne? Doesn't help me much, though."

Even if the damage was reduced, Sally likely still wouldn't survive a single hit—there were basically no situations where she'd lose HP and still live, so the heal over time wouldn't help her, either.

And if it affected an area around Maple—like Martyr's Devotion—then Sally would enjoy the effect anyway since she was usually in the same party, so there was no real point in taking the trouble to get the skill herself.

"For anyone else, Maple, the ability to stack several damage-reduction effects would be invaluable—but everything already bounces off of you."

And Martyr's Devotion allowed her to extend that defense

to everyone around her—so this new skill wasn't all that helpful. Maple didn't need damage reduction or healing over time, either, albeit for different reasons, so she used Heaven's Throne primarily to seal enemy attacks.

"But the visuals are so good! Looks like a real rank higher."

"More wings!"

"If only they let you fly."

"Still have to blow myself up for that."

She tried moving the wings, and they flapped but didn't lift her up.

"Still, it's something. Is that the only skill?"

"Um…like Hydra, it comes with another…and…yup, Twisted Resurrection works on this!"

"Oh?"

"Let's go show the others! It's easier to explain with everyone there."

But she still showed Sally her window, letting her read the description.

"Yeah…good point. You'll mostly be using this when we're all together."

"Exactly!"

"Well, okay. Better put those new wings away. It may not be the strongest skill you've got, but if you bust it out at the right moment there's a good chance it'll make the opposition blink."

"Yeah! Like an ace up my sleeve!"

"Yup, yup. Heh-heh, you're getting the hang of this."

"Eh-heh-heh!"

They were done here, so it was best to head back. They sent a note to any guild member logged in, asking them to stop by the Guild Home, and began their return trip.

* * *

When they opened the door to the Guild Home, they found the rest of Maple Tree gathered.

"You're all here!"

"We got curious. Can't believe you found it already."

"I'm always up for your kind of crazy."

"Should we head to the training room? We want to keep this secret from the other guilds, right?"

"Yeah. We figure we can spook them on first use if we keep it hidden. And Maple doesn't exactly need this skill to fight on her own."

"Makes sense. But…is this gonna spook people?"

"What is it this time?"

"Classic Maple."

She already had a ton of things nobody else had, so there was no predicting this one.

"Heh-heh-heh, you'll find out soon enough!"

They filed into the training room, and Maple stepped forward.

"Just gimme one second…um, I've gotta use that later, so… okay, Quick Change."

Maple first switched to her white armor set for the HP boost.

"All right! Here goes! Glow of Deliverance!"

Once again, the ground glowed, four wings unfurled, and an all-new halo appeared over her head.

"Wow! That's a super pretty skill."

"……Not quite what I imagined."

"Yeah, like…there's all these crazy fish on this stratum…"

And not that long ago, Maple had come back with tentacles. They'd all braced themselves for something far worse and were relieved to find it was just flashy in a regular sort of way.

"Anyone in range gets damage reduction, autoheal, and status ailment resistance!"

"That's…not much help, with you using Martyr's Devotion all the time."

Kanade's opinion matched Maple's and Sally's. Maple's original skill let her soak all damage and status effects for the party, so there wasn't much point in having this new one.

"But at least you look happy about the extra wings?"

"……Fair. Getting those is worth it."

At this point, Maple invited them all to come closer.

"Wait, is there more?"

"Clearly she's not done yet. What is it?"

"You'll find out when I use the skill! Don't worry, it's not dangerous."

Once she was sure everyone was in range of Glow of Deliverance, she used her next skill.

"Okay…Ark!"

She named another skill, and the light on the ground grew brighter. Over the next few seconds, it wrapped around all of them, then lifted them off the ground.

"Whoa!"

"Oh, that's neat. Making us float—is this how Syrup feels?"

Once they were safely in the air above, water began gushing up from below, rapidly filling the training room. The waves wreaked havoc on the dummies, and the glow around the guild members grew brighter still, until they couldn't see a thing.

An instant later, all of them felt a tug from above, then suddenly found themselves on the sidelines of the training room—with no sign of the raging waters.

"Cool, it worked!" Maple said.

The wings on her back vanished, and everything went back to normal.

"Seems handy."

"Yeah, might be useful when we're fighting as a group!"

Having confirmed its function, Maple filled in the others on the skill's effects. Ark could only be used while Glow of Deliverance was active. After a five-second delay, they'd float upward, attacking enemies with a flood. The attack itself was more of a side effect—the movement at the end was Maple's primary goal. Once they were aloft, she could move her party anywhere she liked within the twenty-yard range of the glowing circle.

Ark ended the Glow of Deliverance effect, but that didn't really bother Maple.

"I see… Your defense means the wind-up time doesn't leave us exposed."

"It lets us ambush from cover, or get behind them while they're freaking out about the floor—we can even quickly move out of harm's way!"

It was a one-time effect, so it didn't really fix Maple's fundamental lack of mobility, but it did give her more options in combat, which was never a bad thing.

And all that water was sure to be distracting—if they moved behind their opponents, they could get the drop on anyone seeing this for the first time.

"If I keep it hidden, it may well be very effective someday. It would definitely confuse at first."

"The water does a lot of damage, too!"

"Look at those dummies…"

Maple had been focused on the skill's movement and had barely noticed, but that had indeed been one powerful flood. The training dummies were here for the testing of skills—and they had been chewed up. This would be a real threat to anyone with low defense.

"One more skill to show off! Just a second! Twisted Resurrection!"

This skill altered other skills—and everyone could guess she was using it on Glow of Deliverance. She had them all back off a bit. The original skill might not have meant much to Maple, but it was clearly quite high-level—that much was obvious from her transformation. That meant the altered version would be powerful, too.

"Stay outside the range!"

"Outside?! But the range is huge!" Chrome yelped.

Glow of Deliverance covered just as wide an area as Martyr's Devotion, and if they had to stay outside of it, this was clearly very bad news.

"Annihilation Domain!"

As Maple spoke, black wings unfurled behind her. A halo appeared, glowing dark crimson.

Deep red sparks flew, and the ground turned black and began to glow. Maple's white armor turned pitch-black, and her aura grew sinister. Both the visuals and the skill name suggested none who entered would leave unharmed.

"Maple? What's it do?"

"Um…anyone who steps inside the area will take damage, be more susceptible to status effects, and have healing reduced!"

Basically the opposite of what the original skill did.

"By anyone, you mean party members, too?"

"Yeah…seems like it."

If they stepped in, Sally, Mai, and Yui would die instantly. Kanade and Iz would likely not last long, either.

"……But I do want to see how much it does. And this is a training room…okay, I volunteer! Mind if I step in?"

"Yeah. Chrome, if you could see how much it hurts you, that'll let us predict the effects in battle."

Chrome was a top-tier Great Shielder, and unlikely to die

quickly. He was a good candidate to test the effectiveness of this skill.

"Okay, here goes!"

Chrome stepped forward. Light crawled up him, crackling—and taking HP with it.

"If you're doing damage, then it's not based on your attack stat. Nothing I can't handle, though."

But since it was doing additional damage over time, and interfering with his passive healing, his health pool was steadily diminishing.

"That said, can't exactly afford to hang out in here. This hurts!"

"If it can hurt Chrome, it'll work in most fights. Just having that will keep mages and other squishy targets from getting too close."

"Oh wait, Chrome, I wanna try one more thing!"

"Hmm? Go ahead."

"Okay. Martyr's Devotion!"

Two white wings extended between her four black ones, and a secondary field deployed on the ground. Crimson sparks and gentle white light lit the training room, and Maple had Chrome step back in.

"It might work…?"

When he stepped into the area of effect, the crimson light attacked—but Martyr's Devotion redirected that damage to Maple.

Since she had far more defense than him, she negated her own skill—and the damage he would have taken was completely cancelled out.

Maple could now deploy a domain that would raze everything else to the ground while simultaneously protecting her own party—the best of both worlds.

"Oh, that works! I'm not the only one who can use this!"

"Let's work that into our strats somehow. If we can drop Maple on a line of mages, she could absolutely wreck them."

"What a terrifying thing to have land on you."

"A real heart-stopper."

Maple could now commit mass murder on an all-new scale, so everyone else headed out to the field to look for powerful PvP skills of their own.

---

870 Name: Anonymous Archer
It's all underwater!

871 Name: Anonymous Spear Master
Never done that before, it's rough.
Ain't got Swimming or Diving.

872 Name: Anonymous Mage
At least the diving suits help.
And there's items to give you more air.

873 Name: Anonymous Greatsworder
But when you're underwater...
Fights sure work different.

874 Name: Anonymous Great Shielder
Sally already had both skills maxed so she moves like a fish.

875 Name: Anonymous Archer
Where could she possibly have gotten so many chances to swim?

876 Name: Anonymous Greatsworder
Gotta just grind.
Water fighting may be tough, but it feels fresh.

877 Name: Anonymous Archer
At least arrows still work in the water.

878 Name: Anonymous Mage
How's Maple been?
The water's gotta hurt her, right? She don't have the stats to even get those skills.

879 Name: Anonymous Great Shielder
She's having fun.
If that's all it took to get her down, she'd never have gone full defense to begin with.
Between items and a suit upgraded for max air, she's doing OK.

880 Name: Anonymous Spear Master
Makes sense.
Long as she's enjoying herself.

881 Name: Anonymous Archer
I saw her grinning on the back of a jet ski with Sally, rocketing off into the distance.

882 Name: Anonymous Mage
Iz's logistics game too stronk.
Who else can just make jet skis?

883 Name: Anonymous Greatsworder
I want one!
Think our crafter will learn how soon? Fingers crossed.

884 Name: Anonymous Great Shielder
Can't say.
I ain't an expert, and barely poke my head in her workshop these days.

885 Name: Anonymous Spear Master
She's crafting stuff with mystery techniques.

886 Name: Anonymous Mage
Anyone find anything interesting?

887 Name: Anonymous Greatsworder
Like I said, still on the upgrade grind.
And if I stumbled on a rare event and ran out of breath before it ended, I'd cry all night.

888 Name: Anonymous Mage
True dat.

889 Name: Anonymous Great Shielder
Gotta get your skills and gear in line to even attempt salvage.

890 Name: Anonymous Spear Master
Random lucky dives seem more likely than planning it.

891 Name: Anonymous Archer
You say that! But, hey, Great Shielder!
Your guild is made of people who get lucky their first try!

892 Name: Anonymous Greatsworder
Always.

893 Name: Anonymous Spear Master
The one guaranteed thing in this game.

894 Name: Anonymous Mage
A strategy literally no one else can use.

895 Name: Anonymous Great Shielder
I'm just trying to keep up.

896 Name: Anonymous Mage
Hang in there.
I'm trying to get my own hands on something.
Gotta get the hang of underwater fighting first... Hard to beat fish in mobility...

897 Name: Anonymous Archer
Not without a Maple-level barrage.
Gotta run a party, strength in numbers.

898 Name: Anonymous Greatsworder
If I salvage anything, I'll report it here.

899 Name: Anonymous Great Shielder
Looking forward to it.

 Seeking unknown skills and items, or undiscovered dungeons, the players all plumbed the depths as best they could.

CHAPTER 5

Defense Build and Lost Legacy

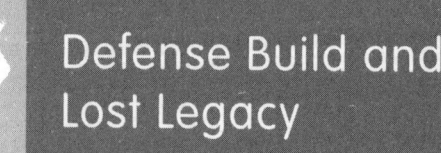

Back out in the real world, the summer sun sure called attention to itself, but at the hour Kaede went to school, the temperatures weren't *that* bad yet.

"Oh, good morning, Risa!"

"Morning, Kaede. It's getting hotter!"

"Ah-ha-ha, it sure is *summer*."

Time had flown. They'd been playing the game for a year and a half now.

They chatted on the way to school, but the topic gradually drifted to their common passion—the game.

"We'll have to find info related to Lost Legacy next."

"Yeah...where could it be?"

"Gonna have to play the long game. Just having the item already gives you an advantage over anyone else. I mean, if you don't even know the item exists, you could be in the right place, and you'd never realize anything was there."

Based on the item's name, they figured it was related to the machines, but anyone without the item itself wouldn't even have known how to narrow things down.

"I found it in the seventh-stratum event…"

"But the destination's definitely on the eighth. That whole last event was setup for the new map."

"Yeah, it did have that water theme."

"Sure helps beat the heat!"

"Just being on the eighth stratum helps you cool off!"

"Yeah…but man, there's eight already?"

"They keep adding more!"

"And they add more stuff to the previous floors with each new stratum. Can't hurt to go scope them out sometimes."

Kasumi had found a lead for her monster pet by swinging through the fourth stratum—one of many hidden elements added after the fact.

Naturally, many of these tied into the new stratum, but sometimes they began and ended on the older maps.

"Lots of stuff is still undiscovered, and the more you explore, the more you find—there's just not enough time to find it all."

Trying to balance exploration with raising your level left everyone pressed for time. Each map was just that large and packed with secrets.

"It's wild! So much to do! Urgh, and we'll have even less time next year."

"Next year…right."

They were both students and would have to hit the books hard next year. Kaede had a good point; Risa's grades weren't especially bad, but her parents were already encouraging her to spend more time studying.

"……Well, we'll cross that bridge when we come to it."

"True!"

It was still summer. No need to worry about it now.

"And you've been diligent enough already, Kaede. I don't think you have to worry."

"Yeah? Shouldn't you be, Risa?"

"Might be hard to believe, but I've been good. No issues here."

"Ah. That's a relief."

"Heh-heh, so right now, I can focus on the game."

And thus they continued their commute—Kaede imagining what the next event would bring, Risa watching Kaede and thinking about the future. Together, they reached their classroom.

Maple and Sally had been among the first to gain new skills, but that didn't stop them from taking out the Jet Ski to search for more.

With their diving suits upgraded, they now had access to the deepest depths. On this stratum, that meant they were finally at the starting line. There was a *lot* to explore down there.

"Naturally, we've got priorities figured out, but ultimately it could be luck of the draw."

"There's so many machines down there!"

Their current goal was finding a use for Lost Legacy. The item name seemed like a hint, so they were focusing on sunken machines and whatever seemed like the remnants of the lost civilization—but had yet to trigger anything that seemed related.

"We've been a bunch of places… It sure is hard to find."

"Hopefully today's our lucky day. This location seems pretty promising!"

Sally stopped the Jet Ski, telling Maple to take a look over the side. Maple popped her face in the water and saw a massive crevasse in the seabed below.

The water was so clear that even from up here she could see

monsters swimming around the top, but the crevasse's interior was a deep blue, and nothing within was visible.

"……*Gasp*! Sally, we're going inside that?"

"Yup. I wanted to hit it up sooner, but apparently it drains your oxygen really quick."

"So that's why we haven't been here?"

Sally would have been fine, but Maple's dive times were entirely dependent on her suit, and they'd needed to wait until she'd upgraded that function.

"Not sure how deep it goes, and I haven't seen any reports on what lies down there. It's pretty dark, so people could easily be missing stuff—and the time limit makes them rush."

"Oof, sounds rough."

"So let's hope we salvage something good."

"Yeah!"

They donned their diving suits, readied Iz's items, and put the Jet Ski away before diving in.

"There's lots of monsters on the way to the entrance. Maple, can you take care of them?"

"Absolutely! Full Deploy!"

Maple was better than Sally against large numbers. She aimed her artillery downward and started firing as the monsters entered her range.

Bullets ripped through the water, laser beams rained down, and monsters that had not even aggroed to Maple yet were riddled with holes, taking massive damage. The attack made them turn to fight, but with elevation on her side and them squarely in her sights, Maple's advantage was unparalleled.

If the monsters approached, the barrage only grew stronger— that meant charging to their own deaths, but on the other hand, staying put made them sitting targets.

"They're pretty helpless."

"I can handle them! Let's keep moving."

"Yeah, we don't have time to spare."

These two just weren't about to bother with any ordinary mobs. Taking out monsters on the way, they dove deeper, reaching the mouth of the crevasse.

"Wow, that's deep!"

This was not a sight you'd see in ordinary waters—the depths of this crevasse looked as if dark blue paint had been mixed into the water. While the water above was clear, visibility here was poor—it was even darker than the hidden route in the submerged shrine.

"C'mon. You'll lose oxygen faster here, so keep a close watch."

"Got it!"

They attached their headlamps and stepped over the rim.

Their feet were swallowed by darkness, and with no solid ground beneath them, the girls dove onward into the gloom.

"Wow… Even night doesn't get this dark!"

It was so dark Maple got carried away, almost forgetting the need for caution.

"Uh…right, Martyr's Devotion!"

The skill generated light and gave her white wings.

"Now I can keep you safe, and you can find me."

"Ah, two birds with one skill."

Not long ago, Maple had turned herself into a signal flare by exploding a lot; this was a much less drastic signpost.

"And since the entrance is at the top of the wall behind us, we should follow it down. That will help prevent ambushes from behind, where our lights won't be pointing."

"Oh! Good point."

Sally was on the lookout, but it never hurt to reduce the risk.

"The monster types should be different, so be careful—I bet they use this darkness to strike."

"Okay! Attacking anything that comes close!"

Since she couldn't see them, she couldn't exactly shoot them down before they approached, but that wasn't actually where these two shined the brightest. They weren't backline mages—close-range combat was their thing. And with Martyr's Devotion active, proximity to the enemy was not a concern.

"It's pitch-black...!"

"If we'd dove down at the center—if we didn't have this wall, we wouldn't even know which way we were facing."

"Especially with the way you fight, Sally!"

Being in the water meant she could dart around in all directions, but in this darkness, she'd lose track of which way she was facing in no time. She might even swim up when she meant to go down.

"Gonna minimize combat unless we hit a boss or something else tough. Which means..."

"Yup, I'm on it!"

"Thanks. We're good to ignore anything trivial and keep moving. Not exactly after the XP here."

"Sounds like a plan!"

They needed oxygen more than experience, so they dove on, fighting only when necessary.

That said, the crevasse was deep and yawning. It did seem like there were fewer monsters near the walls, so they dove a long way without encountering anything.

"Are we actually getting anywhere?"

"I can feel us descending, so...probably?"

The darkness sure made it feel like they were standing still—but then they saw a blue light hovering out in the water, clearly not generated by the lights on their heads.

"Oh, see, we're moving!"

"Is that an item? Or an event?"

"It's not moving, but…Maple."

"What?"

Sally whispered in her ear, and Maple nodded.

"True… If we can't see, better be cautious!"

"Yeah. We're at a disadvantage and may not be able to cover each other."

Ever cautious and ready to reverse if anything happened, they approached the light.

Once they were close enough to reach out and touch it—the darkness *moved*, and their lights caught a row of razor-sharp teeth.

"Maple!"

"Mm-hmm!"

They backed off quick, just before a giant set of jaws snapped shut around their original position.

"I figured that was a lure!"

"You called it, Sally!"

It may have had a skill that let it blend into darkness, but once it opened that mouth, they could see it properly. It was still dark—but the creature's outline was visible.

"Some sort of anglerfish?"

"Probably based on that, yeah. But if we can see it, it's as good as ours."

Sally kicked hard, shooting forward, and swung her daggers at the incoming bulk. Since this anglerfish was all about hiding and chomping, it couldn't keep up with her mobility.

"Deploy Artillery! Commence Assault!"

And at that speed, it couldn't evade Maple's lasers. Bullet after bullet pierced its body—and it turned to light before it could do anything else.

"Nice, Maple!"

"That was easy!"

"If you spot something weird, be extra careful. They might be in disguise. I know you won't fall for *that* one again, but…"

"I've figured it out, yeah."

"But we might get targeted normally, too, so stay cautious."

"Will do!"

They swam for quite a while. The first few monster attacks startled them, but as long as they could see the creatures, nothing posed a threat.

Anything that failed to make an effective first strike under the cover of darkness would find itself at a disadvantage since these monsters had lower stats overall in exchange for their stealth. Getting past Sally's watchful eye *and* actually managing to hurt Maple was such a tall order that it came as no surprise the monsters weren't up to the task.

"We're making steady progress…hmm."

"But still no bottom!"

"How's your air?"

"It's going down, but between the suit and Iz's items, I'm okay!"

"Tell me just before you hit half. No guarantee there'll be a magic circle to get us out."

"Right!"

Since their descent had been careful, their ascent might be quicker—they just had to make sure they could reach the surface. But there was no telling what might happen, so it might be wiser to turn back while they still had the chance.

✳ ✳ ✳

Their dive continued. Since there was no other light, Martyr's Devotion lit up some towering rocks—like a forest made of stone.

"Are we almost at the bottom?"

"First time seeing anything but water ahead of us!"

The bases of these pillars still weren't visible, but it was a change nonetheless. They tried shoving one, but it was anchored fast and didn't budge. Unless these rocks were floating via some mystery power, they must be almost at the bottom.

"……! Maple, over here!"

Just as Maple was sighing with relief, Sally grabbed her hand, pulling her behind a rock.

"Wh-what?"

"……There's something out there."

Maple knew Sally must be right, so she dismissed Martyr's Devotion. They'd never really tested to see if monsters could see its light, but she'd learned it was a good idea to eliminate any chance of detection regardless.

Darkness fell around them once more, and they peered around the rock, squinting into the gloom beyond.

A pale glow slipped between the pillars in the rock forest. It looked like the eye of a creature prowling for prey.

Something huge was swimming about—and clearly not any ordinary monster.

"That was big…"

"Let's try not to get seen. I don't think that's something we're meant to fight. Less a boss than…you remember those snails in the second event?"

"Oh! The ones we couldn't hurt?"

"Right."

If it was just ordinarily tough, they could fight it; if it was undefeatable, that changed everything.

"We only got a glimpse, so maybe we just didn't see the HP bar, but we're short on time to begin with—let's avoid a fight if we can."

"Yeah! Let's stay hidden."

"And this terrain is built for that. I'll notice if it comes our way."

"Okay, I'll trust you!"

"You do that."

With all these pillars, they had plenty of places to hide; it was easy to move around without being detected. Since Sally had spotted its first appearance, she wasn't about to miss its again.

With one eye on the roaming giant, they dove a bit deeper—and as expected, found the floor. Now they just had to search the area. Still, they didn't have that much oxygen left, so they'd have to carefully watch their reserves.

"Should we move out?"

"Can't hug the wall forever. Go time."

They started through the rocky pillars—Sally tracking the monster, Maple keeping her eyes peeled for items or events, ready to use Cover if anything attacked.

"……It's on our right."

"Then we go this way."

Even in the darkness, it wasn't exactly hiding itself the way the anglerfish had; there were signs of it moving. Maple couldn't possibly have picked up on them; however, Sally's detection skills were unrivaled.

There was no telling what would happen if it spotted them, so they avoided all combat—but that meant their exploration slowed to a crawl.

They had no choice, but their time limit was coming up fast.

"Maple, any clues?"

"Nope. I'm seeing nothing. It's big and dark and I dunno where to go."

They couldn't see as far as usual, so there was every chance they'd passed right by their destination.

"It's a hassle, but we'll just have to make several dives."

"But that is very treasure-hunty!"

"…I suppose. Yeah, let's keep coming until we find a treasure. Despite the size of it, no one's reported back, so there's gotta be something here."

Even if this darkness didn't hide an event with a conditional trigger, it was clearly hiding something.

They might spend a while here and stumble across it, and that was its own kind of fun. If Maple was enjoying it, Sally was happy.

"Still, we'd better call it a day soon. No telling how much fighting there'll be on the way up, and something unexpected might happen."

"Yeah, fair. Gonna have to upgrade my suit more…"

Most of her suit's upgrades were done, so it was nearly maxed out, but there were still a few stragglers. It was good enough for most areas of the game, but if they were going to be coming here, she could use all the dive time possible.

Maple checked her air again, and they searched a while longer— but reached the time limit without making any discoveries.

"Urgh, shame!"

"We can always come back. You've got good luck, Maple. We'll find it next time."

"Yeah? Well, that would be nice!"

"Then let's start clim— Wait!"

As they turned, something massive appeared from behind a rock. Sally yanked Maple back behind cover, but they'd been out in the open, and the giant fish reacted accordingly.

"Sally, Sally, the eyes are yellow!"

"......Is it in search mode? Let's hope it doesn't attack directly."

"Is that, like, a signal?"

"Usually. With things like this, there's generally a way to tell how dangerous they are. If its eyes go red, we're in big trouble."

"......Got it."

Exchanging hushed whispers, they waited for the fish's eyes to go back to normal, but there were no signs that it'd change soon. And while they bided their time, Maple was running low on the oxygen she needed for her ascent. Situations like this were exactly why they'd chosen to head up early, which was a good idea…but the situation was only getting worse.

"It's persistent."

"We don't have time to wait it out! Do we just swim up as fast as we can, or try something else?"

Sally was thinking furiously, so Maple ran through her list of skills and items for ideas.

"Sally."

"Got something?"

"If it totally loses track of us, will it give up?"

"Um…definitely a possibility, but how?"

"Remember Ground Cradle?"

They were at the very bottom of the crevasse. One of the few spots on the eighth stratum where you could actually go underground.

"Might be worth a shot. If it doesn't work out, fine. Not exactly a skill we're regularly using here."

They were retreating for the day anyway, so no point saving skills.

"Okay! Then…Ground Cradle!"

At her cry, they both sank into the ground. That completely

freed them from the fish's gaze, but until the skill ran out, they wouldn't know if it had worked.

"Fingers crossed!"

"Yeah. Let's hope it leaves."

Not long after, the skill ended, and they were spit back out. Maple and Sally hugged the nearest rock and scoped out the fish. It was still looming there, eyes glowing yellow.

"Ugh, no use."

"Probably has a timer on it… Maple, how much oxygen?"

"It's pretty low, so……um, huh?"

"What?"

"Sally, it's recharged."

"Er, really?"

Sally checked Maple's oxygen herself, and it had indeed fully recovered. She checked her own.

"Oh, me too."

"Seriously?"

"……I guess that counted as being out of the water."

Their underground visit was the only explanation for what had happened. There'd been so few places they could touch down that it hadn't come up before—but nothing else could have caused this.

"Then we can stay down longer!"

"Unexpected, but a happy stroke of luck. Let's wait this thing out."

"Agreed!"

With Maple's dive time issue resolved, they didn't need to fret about waiting here.

After a while longer, the fish's eyes went back to green, and it resumed its patrol.

"Whoo!"

"It's gone. Whew… It finally gave up."

"Then let's get back to exploring!"

"We're at full oxygen, and coming all the way back would be a hassle. Let's get as far as we can."

Thus Maple and Sally took full advantage of their accidental tank top-up and moved on.

Beyond the stone forest, they hid behind a rock buried in the sand, making sure that giant fish wouldn't come this far. It seemed like that forest was its territory—they waited a while, but never saw that telltale green light.

"Whew, I'm thinking we're in the clear."

"Wonder what happens if it catches you?"

"No clue. But nothing good. We can always check the boards later if you're curious. Someone will likely post the info eventually."

"Ah-ha."

"It's fun finding things out for yourself, but it's also fun reading about what happened to other players."

"I guess I should try that out!"

Maple really only checked the boards for info on how to get skills she needed, or where things were; she never read them for fun.

"There's all kinds of ways to enjoy the game."

"Well, you know more than me. Tell me where to look!"

"Sure, I'll keep an eye out for good yarns. Unexpected twists, dungeon disasters, you name it."

There wasn't much risk of ambush in this new area, so Sally and Maple focused on their search. There was little chance of them missing anything in range of their lights.

"We're coming up empty."

"Yeah, I doubt we missed…"

"What?"

Sally had felt a faint tremor underfoot, and stopped in her tracks. Maple felt the same thing a moment later and turned around.

"Why is…yikes!"

A moment later, sand swirled, almost swallowing her up—and a long-bodied fish like an eel shot out of the sand.

"Guess there was *something*!"

"I'm good! No damage!"

"Cool. But more incoming!"

The eel had shot up, with Maple clasped in its jaws. Sally's headlight located them as she called out a warning.

An instant later, more sand flew up. Giant eels in all directions, each capable of swallowing these girls whole.

"Jeez… Does everything have to be huge here?"

Since the girls were separated, half of the eels chased Maple upward while the other half came after Sally. It was hard to get a proper count in this darkness, but she knew they were coming from all directions.

"Catch me if you can!"

Sand puffed up in Sally's wake, her focus rocketing upward as she dodged incoming eel maws. One bite from those jagged teeth would spell her doom, but a well-timed evasion left them exposed.

"Hahh!"

Taking full advantage of the vertical movement this environment provided, Sally slipped down the eel's flank, gouging it from head to tail with her daggers.

"That hurt, right? Next!"

Each time one came after her, it was left with two spark-spraying slashes.

"Lots of 'em, but this is force in numbers, all big hits. That can't spook me!"

Even in darkness, this wouldn't pin Sally down. If they all

attacked at once, they might have had a shot—but the eels' attack patterns weren't that efficient.

And it didn't take long before crimson flashes started tearing through the darkness, scorching the ground.

"An underwater storm…of lasers."

The eel had carried Maple pretty high up, but all that did was put her in the perfect position. She needed only to point her weapons straight down, descending as she opened up on her foes.

The nonstop laser rain left the eels covered in burns.

No one but Sally could've survived this sort of attack.

"I *could* just focus on dodging them…"

Maple would likely make short work of these eels even without Sally's help, but Machine God's weapons were technically finite. They weren't sure how big this crevasse was or what enemies awaited them—it was better if Sally kept fighting, doing her share of damage.

They didn't want to run out of ammo in a pinch.

Sally kept slashing, and Maple maintained her barrage, gradually carving away the eel swarm's total HP.

It took a while before they started noticeably thinning the numbers, but that didn't matter.

In due time, eel after eel lost all their HP and burst into light. Neither of the girls were targeting individual monsters, so the damage was more or less evenly distributed; once one eel died, the rest of the swarm wasn't far behind.

As their deaths lit up the darkness, Sally saw Maple's headlight descending toward her.

"Welcome back. Nice laser storm."

"I hit a lot of them! I was worried since I couldn't see much."

"Their size worked in our favor."

"Yeah! Whoa… This many sure is spectacular."

The death effects were slowly fading, but since they'd been huge and plentiful, the ocean was filled with sparkles.

"Like marine snow."

"Oh, I've heard of that!"

"Pretty sure the real thing isn't this flashy."

"We got 'em all?"

"This area seems clear. I think they all popped out at once."

Sally called it—when one attacked, they all did, and with the threat eliminated, the girls had earned a respite.

"Doesn't feel like there's anything else here, so let's move on."

"Maybe find some sunken treasure!"

"We'll just have to track it down."

"Fingers crossed!"

Maple took the lead, head swiveling side to side, trying not to miss anything lying around.

The view around them seemed disinclined to change. But since they'd topped up their oxygen, they'd already made far more progress than they'd originally planned.

"How far have we come?"

"Judging from the map, we're about halfway through the crevasse. We've been moving straight ahead, which means we haven't exactly scoured the sides or anything near the walls."

They'd had no clue from above, but the ocean floor had all sorts of terrain. This sandy area was nothing like the initial rocky one.

"This sandy area seems like it's all about ambushes, so I bet our goal is in the next zone."

"But this sand goes on for ages!"

"I suppose the treasure could be buried in it, but we can't exactly search everywhere."

With no clues or guarantees, there was no point in just digging at random. It was hard to prove an absence of treasure, or to know when to quit.

"At least the monsters aren't a problem!"

"Let's just move on. Once you know the trick, attacks from below are easy enough, and we aren't here for the XP or drops."

Declaring the sandy areas useless, they pressed on, eliminating only enemies that came after them until they reached the end of it. Up ahead, their headlights caught the hard surfaces of another rocky zone.

"More boulders?"

"We've got maps, so we definitely didn't get turned around. This is a different rocky area—and these aren't nearly as tall."

"That's true."

"These offer less cover, so I doubt there'll be another giant fish. Unless they just decided to make this one harder."

"You can't be stealthy with nowhere to hide!"

"Let's just be careful. We're wasting oxygen."

"Right! If we dillydally, we won't get to explore much!"

Excessive caution would just work against them, so they swam on into the new zone. Soon, they spotted brick-like rubble lying between the bulky boulders.

"Sally, Sally! What do you think?!"

"Signs that something sank up ahead. Best not spend too much time out here; we'll likely not have much to show for it."

"Agreed!"

"Don't know what monsters might be lurking, so I'm gonna stay close."

"Okay! I'll keep you safe."

"I know you will."

They moved on, looking for clues, and found many signs that

people had once been here. The rubble had once been made from sturdy materials, so it was easy to track the remains.

"I think it's this way, Sally!"

"The number of pieces is increasing, so I think we're headed for the center."

Progress was good. Maple was swimming this way and that, but then she snapped her head forward—and her light caught a shape in the darkness.

"A house!"

"It's collapsed, but…definitely a proper building. Are we nearing a town?"

It did indeed prove to be the outskirts of an abandoned town. As far as their lights could see, all buildings had long since fallen, only a few maintaining recognizable shapes. The volume of rubble alone suggested this had once been a thriving village.

"Let's go in!"

"Yeah, not seeing any monsters."

No reason to turn back now; there was more cover than in the sandy area, so they kept their eyes peeled for ambushes.

"See anywhere we can go inside?"

"Doesn't seem like there's anything under the rubble, so if we find somewhere, that's probably the goal."

"Heh-heh-heh! I'm getting used to ransacking ruins!"

"Oh? Are you sure?"

"W-well, no, but we've done it a lot!"

"True. Certainly we've done a lot of that lately. I bet you're starting to pick up on the clues they leave for us."

Sally figured it was best to let Maple move on instinct, and took it upon herself to pick up any slack.

Maple was motivated and soon found a building she could slip inside.

No doors, no furniture, not even a roof—just the frame of a house, with nothing else of note.

The sheer volume of water had clearly wreaked havoc here.

"Hng, I'm not seeing anything."

"Then let's move on."

"Yeah, forward march!"

One failed attempt would not get them down. They weren't about to give up until they'd scoured every inch of this place.

Maple surged off ahead, with Sally on her tail, making sure they didn't miss anything.

They'd come all this way, and she wanted something to show for it. For Maple, and herself.

They'd been swimming enough to prove there were no monsters here, so they decided to split up to search more efficiently. Naturally, they stayed close enough to see each other's lights and call out to each other.

"Maple! Anything?"

"Maybe!"

"Okay, fine…wait, maybe?"

Sally had almost missed that, but caught it, and swam toward Maple's light.

"Whatcha find?"

"Oh, Sally, look!"

"It's…a stele? Clearly no ordinary rock."

The buildings around it had collapsed, but the stone slab at the center was as black as the water, clearly made of a different material than the rubble and metal in the ruins around them.

"So, what's it say…? Oh."

"I think they're letters!"

The collapse had scraped it, so it was somewhat less than

legible, but the surface of the stele was clearly covered in the characters Kanade had tried to teach them.

"Can you read it, Sally?"

"No, uh…only a bit. Mostly lost on me."

"I was with you, but…ugh, not enough classes…"

Neither girl was slow on the uptake, but you didn't exactly master an unknown language in a single session.

Unless you were Kanade.

"""…………"""

They took one look at each other, and resorted to their only option. Open a window, type in a message—and wait for Kanade to answer.

"What a fascinating find! I imagine it's hard for you to read yet, so I'll help. There's missing bits, but I can work around those. There's something in the center of town. It's important, so it's been sealed away, and it's heavily guarded. I'd say go check it out. And tell me how it goes later!"

"Thank god he answered fast. Sealed away, huh?"

"I wonder what!"

Something "sealed away" probably meant they'd be heading into battle. In which case, their oxygen levels might come into play.

"Maple, can you fight?"

"I've got plenty of skills left! And my oxygen should hold out."

"Then let's hurry up and find the center. Lemme just thank Kanade…done."

With their destination sorted out, they quickly sought the heart of the village, leaving the surroundings for later.

They'd been pretty far into town to begin with, so it didn't take long to find a solid candidate for the center of the village.

"Is that it?"

"Probably."

There stood a building made of the same black stone—like the stele, it had likely been built in the far distant past. Though once tightly secured, years of being underwater had eroded it, and the door was warped, nearly falling off—and certainly not blocking the entrance. It looked like they could easily fit through the gap to see what lay within.

"Doesn't look that big from here. Shall we?"

"The monsters here have all been huge. They wouldn't fit inside this place!"

Figuring there wouldn't be an ambush, they swam on in. They were right—nothing lay in wait. The interior was shrouded in silence.

It went back five, maybe six yards. No signs of any traps.

They followed the wall around but found only a single altar—with writing on it.

"……Ugh."

"Argh! You're our only hope, Kanade!"

No number of remedial lessons would help them here—they had to call in the teacher.

Kanade had expected this writing would show up again, so he'd been on standby in case they sent him more. It didn't take him long to respond.

"Um, we've gotta hit the walls with opposing elements."

"It says that? Okay, I'll do it. You don't have those spells, Maple."

Maple's magic was entirely poison, so this gimmick had defeated her. She might have managed something if items would fulfill the conditions, but…Sally was with her, so she didn't have to try.

Sally could use all kinds of magic, and that was enough to handle this.

"Fire Ball!"

She cast a spell at one wall. The fire itself burst and vanished on contact—but a red magic circle appeared in its place.

"Oh! Success!"

"Yup. Let's try the others."

Sally moved round the walls, casting spells at each. Kanade's explanation had specified which element to use on which wall, so she made short work of it.

When circles were on every wall, the black altar cracked—and blue light shone from within. It shattered, and a sphere appeared in the center of the room, a giant ball of energy crackling like lightning—but nothing else happened.

"……now what? Do we touch it?"

"It looks electric, though?"

"Better put Pierce Guard up. And be ready to dodge."

"Okay! Here goes!"

Indomitable Guardian was still live, so worst-case scenario, they'd have time to bail.

Maple used her skill, and touched the sphere. A moment later, a matching magic circle appeared at their feet, beaming bright.

"C-cover!"

Maple moved to defend Sally—and the light swallowed them up.

The light was blinding, but what had actually happened was a standard-issue teleport. They were spit out into darkness, location unknown.

"Whew… That didn't feel right, so…"

"Mm-hmm, but maybe that's normal for ancient town teleports?"

"It's bad for your eyes!"

"…It's too dark to see much, but there's no water."

"Oh! You're right!"

Maple moved her limbs around, but felt no water. She tried moving up, but fell immediately, like she would on dry ground.

"Then let's take off these diving suits."

"They limit our vision a bit, so that's probably a good idea."

They took off the diving suits and reattached their headlights.

"A proper floor. Same stone as the last place."

"Are we inside somewhere? I don't see a sky."

There was air, but not a star to be seen above them. The floor was man-made, which made it seem more like a building than a cave.

"Should we walk till we find a wall? That might give us a sense of the scale."

"Good idea, let's do that. It's quiet for now, and better to have an idea of our surroundings before anything pops out at us."

They began backing away—bosses had a tendency to spawn facing their starting position, so they went in the other direction.

Before long, they hit a wall. Sturdy black stone, no doors in it, no way out.

"Looks like we're at the far end of it. If we go along it…"

"We might find something?"

"Yeah, and this feels like a boss room."

"I know! Gotta look out!"

It wasn't attacking yet, but the odds were high they'd find something farther in. The sheer size of the place suggested this was one of those bosses that constantly charged at you.

Whatever the nature of it was, they'd rather it wait until they were ready.

This time they tried going sideways, figuring out the width of the room. Their footsteps echoed through the dark. They reached the corner without anything happening.

"It's big."

"Um…and that means…"

"The boss is likely also big."

Boss rooms generally matched the scale of the threat within. This made sense—the boss couldn't really fight properly if it was cramped.

And since this one wasn't underwater, and they had no intel suggesting what sort of boss they might face, it was hard to make predictions.

Once it showed itself, they'd have to make snap judgments about its skills, and wing it.

"We've explored the back, now let's go forward!"

"Be ready for anything, anytime."

"Uh-huh!"

They walked to the far wall, found nothing there, and then went back to where they'd started, this time facing forward.

"Ready?"

"Anytime! Let's do this!"

On guard, they headed into the center of the chamber. The room grew brighter as they did, until they could make out all of it.

Like they'd thought, they were at one end of a massive chamber. The back of it was still a few dozen yards away.

As they crossed the halfway point, they saw crystals and rocks along the walls, plants they'd never seen on this stratum, and what looked like materials.

"Is it a storehouse?"

"But not a very organized one. That thing's got my attention."

"I know!"

Their eyes were on a two-yard-wide black cube, dead ahead.

It was hovering under some unknown force, and was clearly not part of the debris scattered around.

"It reminds me of the underwater thing."

"Monsters like this tend to have limited attacks; this fight may be similar."

The underwater cube had used a lot of water attacks, but this time there was no water. Waiting for it to attack, they took another step—and the cube moved. Blue lines ran across the surface, and its body split apart—much like the altar on the way in had.

"Here it comes!"

"Yup!"

They braced for magic attacks—but when the cube yawned open, out came several stone rods, made of the same material as the cube itself.

These began to spin. There was a crackle, and they began charging energy, eventually releasing a bunch of light bullets.

"A G-gatling gun?!"

"Cover!"

Maple jumped in front of Sally, her shield on her back, soaking the bullets. She took no damage, but the burst effect was so bright she couldn't see ahead of her. The rate of fire was even higher than that of Maple's weapons—ordinarily, you either dodged or were torn to pieces in the blink of an eye.

"This is pretty different, Sally!"

"I thought it would be more…mystical!"

Both the projectiles and the guns firing them were hardly ordinary—it didn't seem like it was going to run out of bullets.

"……Mind if I watch it a bit?"

"Sure! I'm not taking damage, so…"

Sally watched the cube fire away for a while, then nodded, satisfied.

"Okay, I can dodge it. I'll pull the fire, you hit it hard."

"Gotcha!"

If Sally said she could dodge it, Maple was not about to doubt her words. She knew how elusive her friend was—better than anyone.

"Quick Change...here goes!"

"Good luck!"

Sally left the shelter of Maple's back and ran toward the cube. Neither had attacked it yet, so it focused on the closer target.

The bullets were almost hitting her but weren't quite able to track her speed, always whizzing past where she'd just been. She'd been confident she could handle this and was not about to miscalculate their relative speeds.

"Waterway!"

Since this boss was floating, it was harder to strike directly at it than it had been with the underwater cube. Sally's skill finally got a chance to shine again, letting her swim along a current toward it.

If there was no water, she merely needed to make some.

"Pinpoint Attack!"

She thrust her dagger at it, and the blue lines blinked, generating a shield.

"Go through!"

Sally let the skill motion carry her, stabbing the shield. It caught her blow for a moment, with a spark—then gave way, letting her gouge the cube's HP.

"Not quite...a block."

Something about that had felt very wrong, but she didn't have time to stop and look.

Constant motion was a prerequisite for surviving these guns. If she slowed down at all, she couldn't keep the evasion going.

"Commence Assault!"

Sally rode her current away, and Maple's guns slammed the cube's back. She might not match the cube's rate of fire, but she could hit a much wider range. The cube wasn't particularly mobile, so it couldn't flee—it just sat in the path of her return fire.

Like it had with Sally's attacks, the bullets were striking flimsy

shields, making crackling sounds, and then scraping the cube's surface.

"It's working!"

"Good damage, but…"

Thanks to Maple's projectile output, Sally had time to observe the cube's response. She'd never seen an enemy with a second gauge under their HP before—one which rose with each attack.

"Maple! Can you see that second bar?"

"Um…yeah! I can!"

"It's filling up each time it gets hit! Careful!"

"Got it!"

Without knowing what the gauge signified, they just had to step cautiously. At this point, they couldn't even tell if filling it would be good or bad—but they had to empty the HP bar to beat this boss, and that couldn't be done without filling the new gauge.

In which case, they'd just have to roll with whatever it threw at them, and come out on top. Fortunately, these girls excelled at that.

The cube looked tanky, and though Maple's bullets were doing damage, they were a long way from victory. It might have looked like the underwater cube, but that had been a mid-boss—this was clearly of a much higher tier.

"That gauge is almost halfway."

Watching the cube carefully, ready for whatever it did next, Sally played hit and away around the Gatling fire. She never once let the worrying new gauge escape her attention.

And that's why Sally spotted the gauge dropping like a stone—even as attack effects were bursting all around her.

"Maple!"

"……! Cover Move! Cover!"

Minimal words, perfectly understood. Maple warped over to Sally just before the Gatling gun was flanked by two light beam explosions.

"Martyr's Devotion!"

New attacks, so Maple hastily upped her defenses, arms around Sally, detonating her own weapons to gain distance.

"Ah…! Nice, good call."

"Eh-heh-heh! Whoa… What happened?"

They looked back at the cube—and saw two smaller cubes revolving around the main one. While several stone pillars stood at the center of the boss itself, these new cubes each had a single spiked ball floating above them.

"Bombs? I got that impression."

The blast radius had been quite large, and if Sally had to keep evading that, the risk was pretty high.

"Then I'll keep you safe!"

"Thanks. I'll see about protecting your weapons."

Martyr's Devotion could not protect Maple's artillery. For that reason, they'd developed tactics that let Maple keep Sally safe, while Sally shielded her.

"And I bet there's more later. Our attacks build that gauge, then it spends that to create these adds."

"I see!"

Maple was looking at the reduced gauge. No telling how many more weapons this boss could spawn before it ran out of HP.

The boss had high defense to begin with, and those shields were reducing damage and converting it to this other gauge. That meant this boss was far more durable than they'd anticipated.

"This could be a long fight."

"But we're not underwater, so that's no problem!"

"True. I bet this boss couldn't survive underwater, either."

As long as they had the advantage, no use worrying. Sally liked fighting in both scenarios, but Maple had far more options on land.

"I'll stand in front, don't worry."

"No signs of piercing damage!"

The fight was only just beginning. Regrouping, they moved back toward the boss, closing the distance they'd gained.

With Martyr's Devotion shoring up their defense, Maple added Glow of Deliverance in case they needed a quick evac. Sally kept herself in range of those skills so that the Gatling bullets would bounce right off her.

"Keep an eye on the gauge, Maple. Although the added weapons are kinda obvious."

"Will do!"

Once Maple was in range, she generated a giant laser cannon, lowered her stance, and took aim at the heart of the cube. Naturally, stopping to do that meant the bombs and Gatling gun's fire flew her way, but Sally stood in front of her, blocking them.

"Flash Spout!"

Sally generated a geyser to send the bombs flying, then shifted her weapon into a shield, blocking the Gatling bullets with it.

"Commence Assault!"

A red beam shot from Maple's laser cannon, scoring a direct hit on the boss. Naturally—as it had no one standing guard over it.

In response to Maple's laser, the boss's second gauge bounded up—and immediately dropped back down as it generated a new weapon.

"A long barrel!"

"A big gun…? It all looks the same, hard to tell!"

They kept up their attacks, and the long barrel turned toward Maple—leaving a little red light on her forehead like a laser pointer.

"Sniper...!" Sally yelled—

And there was a boom. The bullet hit Maple's head too fast for her to dodge, knocking her all the way back. The lights of Martyr's Devotion and Glow of Deliverance remained, there'd been no red sparks in her wake, and she still had her last-stand skill, Indomitable Guardian—so Sally kept her eyes on the foe, calling over her shoulder.

"If you're fine, start shooting!"

This was not an attack Sally could dodge if she looked away. Whether they could stave this off long enough to get through the boss's remaining HP depended on how freely she could move.

She had Shed Skin left—this was her chance to try things.

"Okay..."

Certain the barrel was charged again, Sally took a step back.

This meant the Gatling gun had to adjust its aim to track her—a brief gap in the onslaught during which Sally was safe to stand still.

The cube was trying to fill that gap—and Sally was trying to bait it into doing so. There was a boom, and the bullet split the air, hurtling toward Sally. But the pointer it displayed first told her where it would go.

"Hahh!"

It felt like time had slowed to a standstill. Sally's eyes could clearly make out the bullet. Half-reaction, half-prediction—her dagger slapped the bullet's side. Sparks flew, and the trajectory light left her brow.

Blocking the bullet with her weapon came with knockback, and sent Sally flying—but she righted herself in the air, landing on her feet.

The bullet itself whizzed over her left shoulder, slamming into the wall behind with a deafening thud.

"Success...!"

The momentary exchange complete, her sense of time's flow went back to normal, and she was off running again before the Gatling gun could get her.

"I *can* deflect them, but definitely better to leave that to Maple."

The gun gave her just enough time to glance at her partner. She'd been right—Maple was unscathed. She'd lost all her weapons, but her HP bar was full.

"Sorry, Sally! You all right?!"

"Yep! You soaked that thing like it was nothing! Very you."

"I'll be ready for it next time!"

She knew the signs now—if Maple had time to prep, she could handle it. She could swallow the bullet whole with Devour or use Heavy Body to negate the knockback. She didn't take damage either way, so there was no worst-case scenario.

"Keep shooting! That's our safest route to down it."

"Got it! Full Deploy! Saturating Chaos!"

"Cyclone Cutter! Fire Ball!"

The girls were dropping a one-sided assault from within multiple safety nets. Without any way to hurt them in return, the boss's HP kept dropping. Without viable strategies against them, all monsters were rendered helpless.

And if they meshed up well, they dominated. A natural side effect of their unusual builds.

"……Two new things!"

"Watch 'em close!"

One of the new things floated up right above the girls. The other stayed hovering at chest-height. The girls braced for anything—and the new devices fired a massive laser from one end of the room to the other.

"Eep?!"

"Whoa, it's moving! Gotta go over or under!"

"B-but how?!"

The laser was sweeping the entire room. Sally could vault over it, but that was asking a lot of Maple.

After all, her flights weren't exactly built for fine adjustments.

"Then…"

"……Gotcha!"

As the laser bore down on them, the Gatling gun rattling on her shield, Sally offered a suggestion.

And it came with a way to bring this long battle to a close.

On board with this plan, Maple detonated her weapons before the laser got to where they were, using the blast to rocket skyward. But not straight up—rather, at an angle.

The sniper (and its knockback) were still charging up, so even if the Gatling gun could shatter the rest of her weapons, it had no way of halting Maple's approach.

"Lure of the Deep!"

At point-blank range, Maple turned her arm into tentacles and wrapped them around the cube. Even with the shields reducing its damage, red sparks sprayed between the tentacles like juice from a ripe fruit squeezed in one's hand.

"It's working! Need more… Deploy Artillery!"

Maple turned her other hand into a giant gun, stuck the barrel to the cube's side, and fired a laser. The damage sparks mingled with the red of the beam, and the boss's HP dropped like a stone—but its second gauge went up just as fast, and it generated a shock wave that sent Maple flying.

"Whoa! Ack! I was so close! Aughh!"

Maple hit the ground and was slammed by the Gatling and sniper gunfire in rapid succession, then her body was bathed in the scorching light of the laser beam as she rolled Sally's way.

"……Still with us?"

"You bet!"

"Appreciate the enthusiasm."

Maple had been right about being close—a few more hits, and they could down this thing. But before they could get back into the action, the boss spent that full gauge, generating the biggest light yet.

When that faded—the Gatling barrels at the cube's center were gone, replaced with a cylinder ten times their thickness. Had they not known better, it would have looked like a stone pillar—but both knew this was a cannon, and a powerful one.

It was already charging up, and the boss generated several layers of light shields in front to protect it.

"What do we do, Sally?"

"We could try and take it down before that fires, but…"

The power and range of this cannon were unknown, but clearly this was the last card it had.

If they could stop it firing at all, that was for the best—but it had also tanked up, and they weren't sure how much.

Dodging into a counter or going all out—both approaches could blow up in their faces.

"Okay, Sally, how's this?"

This time, Maple had the plan. Sally listened, and nodded right away.

"Sure. Let's wait for it to fire, and trust your skill's defenses."

"Okay! They'll work!"

With Maple around, it was better to hunker down—getting hit mid-attack stood the risk of knocking Sally away, out of Maple's protections.

Since any and all attacks could be nullified risk-free with Maple's natural defense and Martyr's Devotion, it was safe to wait for the big gun to fire.

"Any moment now!" Sally said, watching the light grow brighter. She'd taken that as a sign.

"Just in case...Pierce Guard! Unbreakable Shield!"

Skills to help Maple soak the hit. Tentacles gone, she held up her shield. A moment later, there was a high-pitched noise—the gun was ready to fire. With a roar, white light blanketed the entire room.

It was gone in an instant—and no trace of the girls remained upon the scorched ground. In their place—a deluge of water. But that did not mean they'd been defeated—nor had the room cracked, and let the ocean in.

"Perfect timing!"

"Eh-heh-heh! That went well."

They were directly *above* the boss. Ark had moved them just as the laser fired, teleporting them past the attack, without any damage taken.

Those skills Maple used had been a backup plan in case this failed.

The downside of the boss's big gun—the Gatling gun was now gone, and it had no weapons it could turn their way in time. This was the perfect chance to hit it hard.

"Hit 'em, Maple!"

"Okay!"

""Deploy Artillery!""

Each girl turned an arm into a giant laser cannon and pointed its barrel at the boss below. As if matching the cube's ace right back at it, Sally used Reality Twister to make her attack manifest.

""Commence Assault!""

Their lasers mingled, and their combined might was every bit as powerful as the boss's final blast. The beam tore through the boss's shields, scorched its body, and brought its movements to a permanent halt.

* * *

In free fall after the boss's defeat, Sally righted herself, grabbed Maple, and made platforms underfoot, hopping down to the ground below.

"Hokay!"

"Thanks, Sally."

"Good work. Now…that's weird."

"Huh? Oh! The boss is still here!"

Monsters usually burst into a shower of light after being defeated, but this cube was still here—just not moving. Lying on the heap of materials beneath it.

The battle was over. The Machine God parts Sally had created with Hologram and Reality Twister were gone, and a burst of yellow polygons had reverted her clothes back to the default appearance of her new unique series—the set she'd used Quick Change to switch to.

"Lots of things to look into here, so let's go for it. Don't wanna have to come back, right? Not even sure we could."

"True!"

Places outside the ordinary map often had strict entry requirements. Even if you thought you'd followed the same steps, some unknown secret condition often prevented your return—always best to leave nothing unexplored.

Leaving the boss's remains for last, they searched the heaps of junk around to see if they contained anything they could take home with them.

"Hmm. Seeing anything, Maple?"

"Nope! A whole lotta nothing!"

"Guess it's just for vibes. And searching all of it would take ages…"

They'd looked quite a bit but found nothing they could put in their inventories. But knowing there wasn't anything meant they were clear to focus on the boss itself.

"It's not gonna move again, is it?"

"I really don't think so. I mean, there's a magic circle active where we came in."

"True! Then it's probably safe."

The boss was technically no longer a cube—it had split down the middle at the start of the fight, and was still shaped like that.

"Try taking *that* out. Might react."

"Okay! It is similar!"

Maple rummaged through her inventory and took out Lost Legacy. A palm-sized black box, like a mini version of the boss—no obvious difference apart from the size.

"If I hold it close…whoa!"

When she held Lost Legacy up to the cube, a blue line ran across the smaller box. There was a crackle, and a bolt, and it fell from Maple's hand. She reached out to pick it up, but the giant cube made a noise, resonating with it.

"Maple!"

Sensing danger, Sally pulled Maple away. Lost Legacy had been spinning in the air—and the two halves of the boss cube closed around it.

"Whew! I almost got caught by that."

"Best we stay on guard."

"Fair!"

The boss had moved again—so it might be about to resume the fight. They'd cleared dungeons with tricks like that before.

But their concerns proved unwarranted—glowing brightly, the cube began to shrink, ultimately becoming the same size as the box it had swallowed up.

"So less…consumed, more like assimilated?"

"Fused?"

"Maybe so."

When the light faded, Maple picked up the box and looked it over. The name of the item hadn't changed—but there was a new skill on it. And the category had switched from item to equipment.

"I can equip it now!"

"Whoa, nice. You don't have many slots, but…what's it do?"

Maple opened the window so Sally could see, and they read the description together.

Lost Legacy
Ancient Weapon

Ancient Weapon
Stores up energy when the user attacks or is attacked. That energy can be spent to transform it into weapons. More energy must be added regularly to the store, or it will begin to diminish over time.

"So that's what the boss was doing? It spends this 'energy' instead of MP."

"Wanna put it on?"

"Yeah. Better see it for myself."

Maple took off one of her rings and replaced it with Lost Legacy. A mysterious cube—black with a blue line on it—started hovering around her.

"Try attacking."

"Deploy Artillery. Commence Assault."

She began firing her guns at the wall, but the gauge didn't go up.

"Uhh…"

"……No dice, huh? What about getting hit?"

"Then lemme blow myself up!"

Maple lined up some bombs at her feet and lit the fuses. A moment later, a huge explosion left her at the center of a fireball.

Naturally, she knew this wouldn't hurt her at all, but it still wiped the smile from Sally's face.

"Sally! It went up! Already going down, though!"

"Really is meant for mid-combat, then. You're likely meant to build the gauge as you get attacked. You're pretty much the only person who can prep for combat by bombing yourself."

They'd confirmed the gauge would build as she got hit, but this had clearly been designed with more tradeoffs in mind.

Maple spent what gauge she had, activating the skill.

"Ancient Weapon!"

At her cry, the hovering cube stretched to two yards long, then split in two—and Gatling barrels emerged.

"……It's not shooting?"

"It likely autoattacks. And doesn't have a target."

"Aha! But that's nice. I didn't want to carry any more guns."

"Perish the thought."

What kind of Great Shielder had so many weapons she couldn't even carry them? She was too tanky to call herself a gunslinger, but had too much offense to call herself a tank.

"Well, glad we got what we came for."

Further thought on that topic was futile, so Sally decided to celebrate Maple's new skill. The skills and gear they'd found lately were all powerful and could well change the game.

"I'll be even more useful!"

"Nice. Can't wait!"

"Heh-heh-heh… It's gonna be great!"

With newfound strength, they left the place behind.

CHAPTER 6

Defense Build and the Next Event

Time passed. Maple and Sally were enjoying the eighth stratum with their newfound skills and gear.

"I've gotta ask Iz to make tons of bombs so I can use Ancient Weapon anytime!"

"Wonder if she can make ones that don't make noise and have less flashy effects? So you can prep in secret?"

"Blowing a bunch up is pretty obvious! Oh, I could put a gun behind me! Iz makes those cannons."

If she stood in front of her own gun, that alone might keep the gauge filled.

"If you don't mind the visual? Guess the bombs are bad enough."

As they chatted, they were drifting across the waves in a little dinghy. They'd arguably found enough skills, and explored the stratum plenty.

At this point, they had no more clues to follow up on, so it would be hard to find more. For that reason, they'd chosen to kick back and relax instead.

"Oh, there's gonna be news on the next update today."

"Really?!"

"Yep...should be soon."

Even as she spoke, they got the alert signaling a new message. It proved to be from the admins, and about the next update.

"Um...the ninth stratum's next! That was fast."

"It took pretty much the whole time to get the suits upgraded, really. Plenty left unexplored, but that's always been the case."

And it never hurt to circle back into the previous floors. Early finds like Hydra and Devour were still very useful, so what they found down below might come in handy.

If you were in the mood, it never hurt to wander.

"Oh, and they've got news on the event they're holding after the ninth stratum unlocks."

"Um...a large-scale PvP event, dividing us into two camps?"

"Pretty sparse on details, but...your new skills oughta help."

"Yours, too!"

"I've been practicing tricking people."

To make full use of her new skills, Sally had to simulate a bunch of use cases and figure out how to react to them. Just activating the skills didn't make them inherently powerful.

"The dungeon to the ninth floor is nearby, so wanna go scope it out? No use clearing it until the update rolls out, of course."

"Sure! Curious what that area's like."

Many places they'd gone had involved more than simply diving down. If this one looked like a lengthy dive, they'd need Iz to craft more items.

Since they were in the area already, they didn't even switch to the Jet Ski—they just rowed over. They soon spied their destination, and Maple started nodding.

Before their eyes was a long, thick tower that stretched to the very bottom of the sea. The tip was above water, and beneath the waves there were many signs of expansion to escape the rising sea

levels. Naturally, the farther down you went, the more crumbled and eroded it became.

"We go down this?"

"Looks like. Doubt we can shortcut through a gap in the side."

The tower might be in ruins, but there were no windows or holes in it—no ways to skip the dungeon.

"Let's all go together!"

"Few things can defeat all eight of us."

"We're all strong!"

They'd have their work cut out for them finding a viable threat these days. Even if a monster like that existed, there was likely some trick out there to weaken it first. Otherwise, no one playing would ever stand a chance.

"Guess we'll tackle this another time… Hmm?"

"What's up, Sally? Oh!"

Maple followed her gaze to the sky, and saw two shapes above. One was a dragon, whose white scales glittered in the sunlight. The other was a phoenix, whose wings burned as bright as the sun itself.

"Mii! Pain!"

"Maple, fancy seeing you here—but I suppose it's to be expected. I imagine we all saw the same message and came to scout the place out."

"Yup, yup. You doing the same, Mii?"

"More or less. I had business to take care of out here, so it was on my way."

"Pain, you also checking out the dungeon?"

"Yeah, I've been focused on the ocean floor, and hadn't cleared this yet. We'll all need to clear it, so the more I know about it, the better a grasp I'll have on the strength of any player who can survive it."

Rumors spread fast—soon after they reached the ninth floor,

people would start bragging about how they'd cleared the dungeon leading in. The more you knew about the dungeon ahead of time, the more those stories would tell you about the braggart's skills.

It was much easier to deal with threats when you could make educated guesses.

"For PvP?"

"Naturally. We'll be split into two camps—and if we're on opposing sides, I look forward to a rematch."

Since the fourth event, they'd cooperated—but had no chance to fight head-on. Maple and Sally had each grown far stronger, but Pain likely had as well.

"W-we'll do our best!"

"Whether friend or foe, I always bring my A game. If we fight, this time, the Order will win."

"Flame Empire feels the same. You burnt us pretty bad, but rest assured, that will not happen again."

"Well…we're not about to lose! Let's all make it a good one!" Maple managed.

Both Mii and Pain grinned—that was what they'd been hoping to hear.

"Then I'll take my leave. Looking forward to the next event."

"Maple, should we meet in battle, I'll demonstrate my might."

With that, Pain dove into the dungeon, and Mii flew off across the ocean.

"I guess we could end up fighting again."

"They're strong. Both of them have far more to offer than what we witnessed in the eighth event."

It had been a long time since they'd had to fight either of them. Both were higher level and had far more skills. Pet monsters alone could make all the difference, and both of them had tamed truly spectacular creatures.

This would hardly be a repeat of last time.

"We'll have to start scheming. You've got a lot more skills, Maple. Any one of which could turn the tide of battle if used right."

"I'll help you plan!"

"Oh, yeah? Sweet. You're the one who has to use them, so best if our plans make sense to you."

The more she played, the more Maple was getting the hang of things. She had a pretty good sense of what actions worked for her, now. And that allowed her to dream up new ideas.

"Your plan saved us in the Lost Legacy dungeon…so I'm all ears. I've always wanted to strategize with you."

"Ah-ha-ha…there was a lot of luck involved with *that* idea."

Her first time using Ark in battle, and she'd had no clue when the enemy laser would strike—luck had definitely been a factor in choosing when to act.

"But I've seen how you use Spirited Away to dodge attacks, so I thought I could do the same."

"If we practice, I'm sure we can make it yours."

"Yeah? Worth a shot!"

"……It would certainly help. I can see that being a big part of our schemes."

"Eh-heh-heh! Then I'll do my best!"

"Sounds good."

Maple seemed optimistic, so Sally grinned back.

Floating near the tower, they chatted a while—but Pain and Mii were not the only players stopping by. Since everyone would have to clear this dungeon once, lots of players wanted to check it out, just as Maple and Sally had.

"Are we in the way?"

"I doubt it, but it's not a great place to discuss our plans."

Any strategies discussed here were an open book.

As they considered moving on, they saw more familiar faces approaching.

"Damn, you called it!"

"But of course. Will would hardly mistake *them*."

It was the leaders of Thunder Storm and Rapid Fire. Wilbert had likely used a skill to spot them from outside their visual range.

"I do beg your pardon. We just happened to be close by."

"PvP! Like, finally!"

Wilbert bowed his head, but Velvet was clearly champing at the bit.

"True," Sally said. "They did keep us waiting."

"Exactly! Co-op is like, fun and all, but I sure as hell hope we're enemies this time!"

Velvet didn't mince words, and both girls looked taken aback.

"……She's feeling competitive," Hinata ventured.

"Events are our one chance to fight each other! Why wouldn't we wanna throw down?!"

The system did allow players to fight each other in duels, but the tension and triumph could hardly compare to a one-time-only event. Maple might not have understood that, but Sally was well aware of the discrepancy.

"Well, if we're gonna be enemies, we'd best come prepared," she said.

If they had a choice of camps, Velvet would undoubtedly choose the other one. If there was no chance of them ending up allied, they'd best have counterstrategies in place—and more thorough ones than for Pain and Mii, who hadn't picked a side yet. Seeing Sally working that angle already, Lily chimed in.

"I like your attitude. Oh, I should say our guild doesn't have strong feelings either way. Yet."

"……Most guilds don't," Hinata said. "Even if they have a preference, few need announce it to the world the way Velvet has."

She was poking Velvet in the ribs—their guild would likely yell at her later for talking too much.

"That said, whichever side we wind up on, we will be playing to win."

"But of course. If we are on different sides, let's have fun with that."

It had been a long time since there had been a proper PvP event. Everyone was conscious of how much they'd improved, and with this event not due till after the ninth stratum came online, they'd be feeling each other out for the duration.

"Then it's on!"

"You got that right! This won't be like our duel—I'll have Hinata with me! Victory is mine!"

Fighting together, each was far more powerful. Maple and Sally had seen that firsthand. Sally may have won her duel with Velvet, but she knew the Thunder Storm's leader was better than that.

"It's a ways off, so I'll have to keep improving my archery."

With what they knew now, there was no telling whom you'd be fighting with or against. All they could do was improve their skills and gather information.

"You're tackling the dungeon next, Velvet?"

"Hell yeah! Running it with these two."

"We're hardly about to pass on a chance to see them fight up close."

Hinata made a face at that—Velvet herself was likely not thinking about gathering info at all, but she never was, so Hinata had given up trying to convince her otherwise.

"You two wanna come? We'd love to have ya!"

"What do you say, Maple?"

Maple thought for a minute, then said, "Um, I'd rather wait and run it with the rest of our guild. Sorry!"

"Right on! We'll just have to play together some other time."

"Yeah! Sounds great!"

They waved the four of them off into the dungeon, like they had for Pain before them, and began to row their boat away.

"Everyone's got their eyes on the next event, huh?"

"Fighting monsters and exploring is fun and all, but fighting other players is a vital component."

"You're good at that, Sally."

"……Yeah, and it's fun for me."

Like Velvet said, only events raised the stakes so high that the outcome truly mattered. It made sense this would motivate people.

"Gotta explore the ninth stratum, and get ready for the event!"

"…………"

"Sally? What's up?"

"Hmm, oh, just…thinking about plans. Really, we can only do so much until we get the full details."

Right now, "huge PvP event" was basically all they knew about it. It could be a capture-the-flag deal like the fourth event had been—or it could be more of a battle royale.

And those terms would change their strategies.

"No use fretting over it now. Gotta get to the next floor first. Knowing you, Maple, you'll likely get even stronger before the event begins."

A new stratum meant tons of new quests and dungeons. Those could send Maple into all-new dimensions of power. The odds might be low—but the monster before her had been born by fluke, and had grown through luck alone. Sally could hardly say it would not happen again.

"I'll certainly try!"

"And I'll work on mastering my new skills."

With a rough deadline in sight, Sally wanted to adjust to fighting in her new unique series gear as much as possible. She wouldn't be fighting monsters—she'd be fighting the best players in the game. So far, all she'd done was use Hologram and Reality Twisted to copy Maple's skills and to shapeshift her weapon. But she needed to bring *all* these skills into play.

"We should head back."

"Yeah! Surprised so many people showed up."

They weren't here to clear the dungeon—just get a sense of the vibe and size, and to pinpoint its location.

Sally resumed rowing. This was a much more leisurely trip than the Jet Ski provided, so Maple took out a fishing rod, dangling a line over the side.

"Heh-heh-heh… Think you'll catch anything before we get back to town?"

"M-maybe one!"

Maple's fishing skills were the same as always, so the time between her catches had yet to improve.

Sally rowed slightly slower, hoping that would let Maple land a catch.

A relaxing time—yet Sally's mind was elsewhere.

"……Our one chance to fight each other, hmm?"

She echoed Velvet's words, speaking to no one in particular—and so her words were drowned out by the splash of her oars.

CHAPTER 7
Defense Build and the Ninth Stratum

After some time, the ninth stratum's launch arrived. The members of Maple Tree gathered, planning to tackle the tower to the depths below.

"One big benefit of this stratum: my Swimming and Diving skills leveled up."

"It'll be nice if I can use them on the ninth stratum."

"Endings come so soon! But I'll probably have to come back if I want to craft anything with the water element."

"Ugh, I wish we could have learned Swimming!"

"But we don't have the stats..."

"Well, you'll get to make up for it today. It'll help me out if you can make short work of this boss."

""Okay!""

"Right, then should we get moving?"

"Ready, Syrup?"

If they all wanted to move together, Syrup was best—the turtle could ignore any and all terrain.

Maple made her pet giant, and everyone climbed aboard its back. Together, they flew toward the tower.

"We rode Haku around a lot on land."

"But being able to fly sure is useful."

Since this stratum was all about underwater monsters and dungeons, the sky was monster-free, and their flight was a peaceful one.

The eight of them reached the tower without incident.

Maple guided Syrup to a stop nearby, and they dove down to the tower. She put the turtle back to regular size—if Giganticize was active, it couldn't exactly fit.

With everyone ready, and Martyr's Devotion going, they clustered around Maple. The top level of the tower was *not* underwater—just a floor a few dozen yards wide, with a wooden trapdoor set in it. Lifting that door would lead through the ceiling of the level below.

"So it's not intended to keep the water at bay?"

"No monsters here—we're clear to descend."

The lack of monsters here suggested it was still just part of the entrance.

"For safety's sake, I'll stand over here!"

Maple moved next to the door, creating a cylinder of light that blanketed the area.

"Opening it up!"

Chrome opened the door—there were no windows, and it was dark below. They shone a light down, and found it was not yet flooded—but there *was* something moving.

"……Did you see that?"

Maple's defensive field reached the space below, but an iron ladder was the only means of descent—it would be hard for them all to go together.

"I could carry Mai, Yui, and maybe Kasumi and jump in…"

"……But we've got height on our side," Iz grinned.

That gave them *options*. Realizing what she meant, Chrome decided that was safer and elected not to jump in.

What happened next was just mean. A stream of bombs dropped through the lone entrance to the floor below, followed by fire-generating crystals—then the party slammed the door closed.

"Cover your ears!"

A moment later, there was a deafening boom and the entire floor shook. The wooden door's object class meant it neither shattered nor flew open—so the floor they were on was unaffected. However, it was unlikely that anything below had survived.

"……Positioning is everything, huh."

"You can say that again."

"Let's rinse and repeat for now. Rethink it if there's water."

Several floors were annihilated by Iz's room-wide explosions, pulverizing the monsters so fast they didn't know what hit 'em.

"……You really can't let Iz get on top of you."

"Wow! This keeps us all safe and sound!"

It's often said that offense is the best defense—if they blew up all the monsters before they could attack, this place was a breeze.

"Uh…looks like the end of that ride. This floor's flooded."

"Aw. Then these bombs won't work."

"And it's getting darker. Some big fish swimming around."

"Should we switch to diving suits? Have Mai and Yui go buck wild?"

"I'll keep you safe on the way in!"

"Cool, let's do it."

With Maple coming along, nothing could hurt them. Just in case, Chrome led the way, with Mai and Yui right behind.

They dove into the water, and the fish turned and charged in, sharp teeth bared.

"No time to worry about me, girls."

""Quick Change!""

As the fish converged on Chrome, Mai and Yui got their eight hammers spinning.

Each one contained the concentrated force of *all* Iz's bombs.

They were just waving them about—these were *regular* attacks. But the power of each hit dwarfed most players' ultimate moves.

All a hammer had to do was clip a fish and it would burst into light. Their simplistic violence surged through the room, demolishing everything in their wake.

"Whew…they're in our party, so I know it won't hurt even if I do get hit, but it's still nerve-racking."

Mai and Yui were also being careful not to hit their friends, but if an all-destroying heap of metal shot past your eyes, you'd flinch, too.

"Amazing!"

"That went well!"

"Thanks for the defense, Maple!"

"Eh-heh-heh! You don't even need it now!"

Still, it was a relief to know they'd be okay if an attack happened to get through the hammers. Chrome heard this, and nodded—that safety net was what Great Shielders were for.

"I see it went well."

"Oh, Sally. Yeah, once they get spinning, trash mobs are toast. And the fact that Martyr's Devotion works vertically is plain broken."

"Yup."

The diameter was broad enough to cover the width of the entire tower, so if any monsters here wanted to mess with them, they'd have to get past Maple's DEF first. That was too high a hurdle—everyone here assumed it was outright impossible.

"Okay, let's keep moving! I'll let you all handle offense."

When all eight of them were around, there was no need for

Maple to fight. She was better off hanging out with a potion in hand—in case of unexpected damage. As long as Maple stayed standing, their formation would never collapse.

They'd switched from the Iz plan to the Mai, Yui, Kasumi, and Sally offensive, going down, down, down. If the monsters were quick, Kasumi and Sally handled them; if they had lots of HP or defense, Mai and Yui overcame them.

Chrome drew aggro and used Necro's AGI debuff skill. Nothing here really gave them trouble.

"Great work. We don't really need to help."

"Heh-heh… I'm fine with hanging out in back. Keeping my shelves filled."

"There's more of them now? Can you even run out?"

"Hmm…who knows!"

"Kanade, if you ran through all those books, it would be one hell of a battle."

"Ha-ha-ha, true. I'll use them if I need 'em."

Maple and Iz could not imagine a foe that would require that.

As they were talking, Sally popped her head up from below.

"Done! Next floor's a big drop down, so we're thinking everyone should go at once."

"Gotcha!"

"So it's like several floors tall? I'll get ready to use my grimoires."

"Yeah, good idea. Hard to tell with no windows, but we're pretty deep now—might be boss time."

Once they were all together, they headed down. The next few levels had no floors remaining, just the exterior walls. From the bits left along the edge, it seemed less like the waters had eroded the floors and more like something huge had shattered them.

"That's deep! Gonna be hard to reach the bottom."

"But since it's not split in floors, you could call it a time-saver."

"……Did you see that light?"

As they peered down, Sally spotted something glimmering in the depths. As their eyes locked onto it, three glowing clumps of water flew their way one after the other.

Sally and Kasumi evaded quickly, and Chrome caught one on his shield. Iz and Kanade managed to dodge, but the twins had always been slow, and didn't have the Swimming skill—so they couldn't pull it off.

When the orbs hit, bubbles and effects burst around them. Martyr's Devotion meant the damage went to Maple, so they all looked at her.

"…No damage! But my air…!"

Each hit had taken a chunk out of her oxygen reserve.

"Yikes, that *is* bad news."

"How mean! A long dungeon with an enemy that targets your dive time?"

Given the shift in decor and terrain, it seemed safe to assume this was the boss.

But they were still too far up to see it. It was just firing from the bottom, its range far longer than their own.

"If your shield's up, you'll be fine! Maple and I'll lead, guarding as we dive. If we take too long, Maple's in trouble!"

"Agreed. I'll ready a defensive spell."

"I'll deflect with my blade. I've got Mind's Eye; I can see the attacks coming."

"I could shift my dagger to a shield, too?"

"Mai, Yui, we'll keep you safe, so when we get there, give it the ole one-two."

""Will do!""

"Okay. Move out!"

At Maple's cry, they began their dive. They moved the twins to the back and the Great Shielders to the front, shoring up their

defenses. Iz and Kanade provided support, and Kasumi and Sally hung out on the front lines, ready to fend off attacks.

"Four shots!"

"All yours!"

"I'll take one!"

Kasumi swung her katana, and just before it hit, the water burst into bubbles.

For safety's sake, Sally had turned her dagger into a shield, blocking with that. Maple and Chrome took the remaining pair—not one scored a direct hit.

""Thank you!""

"Division of labor!"

"Yep, best player for the job. You two focus on this boss."

Handling orb after orb, Kasumi and Sally noticed a change in the water around them.

"The current... Kasumi!"

"Mind's Eye!"

Kasumi's skill would let them turn Sally's hunch into fact. Her eyes saw everything by the walls blanketed in red—the hitbox of the incoming attack.

"Hug the walls! This is big!"

While Mind's Eye was active, Kasumi was never wrong. Her words came true mere seconds later.

They'd barely made it out of the way when a huge current ripped up the center of the room. Getting caught in that would have hurt—and swept them back to the start position.

"Edges are next! Back to the center!"

"Kasumi, can you keep it going?"

"......Yeah, Specter of Carnage, Mind's Eye."

A red aura appeared around Kasumi, reducing all her cooldowns. This let her use Mind's Eye again right away.

"Once this runs out, I can't use any skills, but with the twins around, we won't need them."

Even with the skill's penalty putting all her moves on cooldown, keeping the twins safe was still for the best.

No attacks got past Kasumi when she was in this state.

She could see the future and dodge any attack, even those that came without warning. Reliant not on experience or instincts, but on facts that Kasumi would not misread.

As the second current passed by harmlessly, Specter of Carnage ran out, and Kasumi's vision went back to normal.

"Out of time… The rest is up to you."

"We're pretty far down. We should see it soon…"

Peering into the darkened depths, they saw a huge number of lights—like the starry sky.

They knew what *that* meant.

"Give us a barrier!"

"Sou, Awaken, Mimic, Guard Magic."

Kanade and Sou *both* deployed barriers, and Iz threw out some crystals that generated a crackling energy barrier.

Those lights in the depths were a barrage of water bullets. It was a curtain of fire impossible for Maple Tree to evade. But the barriers placed in their path held out—and once again, they avoided a direct hit.

"……Boss sighted!"

Sally was out in front and finally got a clear view. A massive fin took up the bulk of the tower's base, beautiful white scales gleaming. It was more of a water dragon than a fish.

Spotting their approach, the dragon stirred to life, ascending at tremendous speed.

"……! Don't let it get past us! That'll let it fire on us from above!"

If it knocked them aside and got through, they'd have to repeat this whole process, this time in the other direction. That was likely

an unavoidable event for anyone else—but this party needed only a momentary opening.

"Sou, Slow Field!"

"Necro, Dead Weight!"

Sou made the space before them warp, and Necro's skill made a giant skull appear behind Chrome—both slowed the water dragon's advance, reducing its speed.

"Lure of the Deep!"

Maple's tentacles spread out wide. One of them struck the dragon's body, generating a shower of damage sparks. But that was not the skill's true purpose, merely the side benefit Devour provided. The tentacles' primary effect was another thing entirely.

There was a *bzzt*—and the dragon was momentarily paralyzed. It was a boss, so the status effect only lasted a second.

One whole second.

And in that second, it didn't move at all—which was more than long enough for the twins.

""Double Impact!""

Sixteen hammers struck home with dizzying force. This boss had no weird resistance gimmick. It was no raid boss. It could not withstand that overwhelming power.

Sixteen impacts rippled through it…and the boss's HP vanished in the blink of an eye.

With the boss downed, they dove silently through the remainder of the tower's interior, well aware that a magic circle to the next stratum waited at the bottom.

"Good work! Now we know our oxygen will last!"

"Great. That paralysis was perfect, Maple."

"Not often that aspect of the tentacles comes into play."

"Probably 'cause they kill most things before it kicks in."

"True…"

Clearing this dungeon meant leaving the world of water behind for now.

And their air was limited—better not hang around talking. The eight of them stepped onto the transport circle.

"Wonder what it's like!"

"Guess we'll find out."

They were wrapped in light, and when they could see again, there was solid ground underfoot. They removed their diving suits and gazed out at the view before them.

From this hill, they could see two distinctive elements.

On one side—water and ice. On the other—fire and lightning. As if signifying light and dark, one side sported rich forests, with liberal use of white, while the other side sported lava pools amid pitch-black rocks. At a glance, they were clearly polar opposites.

Furthermore, in the distance they could see a major town in each direction.

"Aha! I get it. This explains the two camps thing."

"Yeah, it's very obvious."

"Do we pick sides as a guild, or as individuals?"

"Mai, which would you prefer?"

"Er, um…the forest side seems safer…"

Everyone had their own thoughts on these new landscapes.

"Maple, what do you say? I bet we've gotta pick one or the other. Side with light, or side with dark."

Maple's skill tree leaned toward the latter—but she'd picked up several light-side skills on the eighth stratum.

"Hngg, I'd have to look around first."

"Guess that's an option. Can always pick a side for the event itself."

Before that happened, they could explore all over.

The forest side featured beautiful views. But the more dangerous-looking side with rocks and lava seemed more likely to feature things they hadn't seen before.

That left Maple unable to make up her mind.

"Okay! Let's just go see what they've got!" Maple cried, excited to see what this stratum had to offer.

---

350 Name: Anonymous Spear Master
PvP at last!

351 Name: Anonymous Archer
Time to prove how strong we got.

352 Name: Anonymous Greatsworder
Still no deets, but I sure don't wanna get eliminated fast.

353 Name: Anonymous Mage
I'm certainly stronger, but the monsters are way worse.

354 Name: Anonymous Great Shielder
Doesn't sound like it's 1-on-1 so positioning'll matter.

355 Name: Anonymous Mage
Says the man from the monster house.

356 Name: Anonymous Great Shielder
No idea who you're talking about.

357 Name: Anonymous Greatsworder
Well? Anything go down on floor eight?

358 Name: Anonymous Great Shielder
Lots, but that's all I can say.

359 Name: Anonymous Spear Master
Y'all just keep doing what y'all do.
We already know wassup.

360 Name: Anonymous Archer
Weirdness isn't supposed to be that common.
Right....?

361 Name: Anonymous Mage
Well, end up on the opposite side for this PvP, and you'll find out firsthand.

362 Name: Anonymous Greatsworder
Spare me the atrocities.

363 Name: Anonymous Spear Master
What if she goes from one tentacle arm to full-body?

364 Name: Anonymous Archer
After all that time underwater?
Wouldn't be shocked if she added a few more tentacles, no.

365 Name: Anonymous Great Shielder
I'd just think it was very Maple.

366 Name: Anonymous Spear Master
Our last boss.

367 Name: Anonymous Archer
Monster + Person ÷ 2 with a pinch of angel
"served with tentacles"

368 Name: Anonymous Greatsworder
Don't forget the side of artillery.

369 Name: Anonymous Mage
Unappetizing.

370 Name: Anonymous Great Shielder
When the meal eats you.

371 Name: Anonymous Spear Master
Eating players like it's normal.

372 Name: Anonymous Archer
There's a chance she *didn't* get stronger!

373 Name: Anonymous Greatsworder
That's just wishful thinking.
I wonder what the truth holds?

374 Name: Anonymous Great Shielder
You'll have to see for yourselves.

375 Name: Anonymous Mage
If we go up against her? I mean, part of me wants to see it up close, but...

They'd find out when Maple showed off her stuff. This was true for more players than just Maple.

Maple Tree was enjoying their time here, exploring the ninth stratum—as were their rivals in the Order of the Holy Sword, Flame Empire, Thunder Storm, and Rapid Fire. All awaiting the start of the PvP event.

BONUS STORY

Defense Build and Deep Thoughts

Lily and Wilbert were rowing across the lapping waters of the eighth stratum.

News of the ninth stratum had just broken, so they were making their way toward the dungeon that led to it.

"Lily, ahead of us…"

"Ha-ha-ha, I can hear her myself. She never fails to impress."

Lily was rowing, so she was facing backward. She turned, glancing over her shoulder at the source of the noise. It was a bright, sunny day. The sky was blue save for a few fluffy clouds…and the lightning streaking across it.

The whole storm was moving, so they knew it wasn't an eighth-stratum event.

"They're coming our way."

"Ah. Then…let's wait for them."

"Indeed."

As the lightning abated, two girls emerged from within. Velvet and Hinata, from Thunder Storm.

"Your skills are certainly a spectacle."

"Hmm? Oh, damn! Lily!"

"Fighting again? I doubt any monsters here will pose a threat to you."

Most fish tried to gain the advantage by darting about in the water, but this was useless against Velvet's AOEs. Didn't matter how fast they approached—they'd still wind up fried.

Sensing this conversation would continue, Hinata took out a boat and set herself and Velvet down on it.

"Oh…like, thanks!" Velvet said. "Yeah…they're not giving me much of a challenge. But with PvP coming, I can make do!"

It was easier to find strong players than strong monsters. By the time people reached the eighth stratum, they were off on a path all their own, and that had led many people to power.

"Ah, the next event? Dividing us into two camps means the scale will be much larger than the guild wars were."

They didn't know much more than that for now, but it was easy to imagine multiple guilds working together.

"Exactly!"

"I was just thinking about starting discussions on possible alliances. We're hardly the guild you most want to battle, yes?"

"……Velvet, what do you think?" Hinata asked, clearly delegating the decision.

Velvet had to think about that one. "Hmm…we already went all out once."

"Ha-ha-ha, indeed we did."

"So we're well aware of how strong you are," Wilbert added. "Worth considering the proposal, at least?"

Velvet nodded. "You got a point there! Loads of other people I'd rather fight."

"……And this might earn you some points with the guild?"

"True! Gotta do something besides give 'em headaches."

If they teamed up with Rapid Fire, they'd be a major player in this next event. There weren't that many huge guilds out there—and they were two of the best. The ideal alliance candidate. Her guild members were unlikely to object.

"Naturally, we're not locked in to this now. I am planning on speaking with a few others in due time."

Lily was giving them an out to refuse later, but there was value in speaking of this now.

"You both, like, got stronger?"

"What do you think, Will?"

"We're certainly higher level. And it's not like we're lacking for new skills. So…"

"Heh-heh, there you have it."

Maple Tree was not the only guild that had benefited from the eighth stratum's secrets. Many players had managed to salvage *something* from the ocean depths.

"Ah-ha! Sweet!"

"How did you fare?"

"I didn't get all that much. A few of my guild members did good. Hinata's find was off the charts!"

"Oh? Well, we don't want to face *that*."

"Where you two headed?"

"We planned to scope out the dungeon to the ninth floor."

"Care to join us? Might be worth getting a sense of each other's strength before we form this alliance."

"I'm in, hell yeah! Hinata, you come, too."

"Sure…but…I might not use my new skills."

"In that case, let's get moving. We can talk more on the way."

And thus, the four headed toward their destination.

The news of the new PvP event sent ripples through the other guilds. Guilds that posted good results were marked by one and all—and factored into battle plans. No matter the player, the right skills could make a world of difference. Maple was living proof of that.

This game had all kinds of skills, and the right combination could flip the charts.

Naturally, the top guilds were doing whatever they could to prevent that. The Order of the Holy Swords were acting like defending champions.

"Frederica, any good intel?" Dread asked.

"Some, yeah. But the eighth stratum's underwater, and like I keep saying…not my forte."

Frederica sounded frustrated. She could boost her speed with magic, but her core stats were very much backline mage—many players could easily outrun her.

This didn't seem to bother Pain. "Every little bit of information helps. And the ninth stratum will be here before the event. That may prove critical."

Once they reached dry land again, they'd start to *use* what they'd gained in these waters. Learning just how strong the other players were would make a big difference in this camp war. Like Lily was doing, powerful players would track each other down and form alliances to give their side an advantage.

"Yeah, I'll have to make up for it there!"

"PvP!" Drag said. "Gonna be even bigger than the guild wars, yeah? Sounds brutal."

Dread hit back at that. "Frederica will help there. All those buffs!"

"Please tell me you're all better at fighting armies now!" she wailed.

"You saved us in the last event, and I'm sure you will this time, too."

"That's my job, I'll do what I can."

"But what's the plan, Pain? With only two camps, best we start making deals."

"Yeah! The more we got backing us, the better!"

"Naturally, I intend to do just that. But…ideally, we'll have the power to turn the tables all on our own."

"You do dream big!"

But all three knew Pain meant it. If they could consistently win without help, then that was the purest form of strength they could find.

"All right. I can dig it."

"I'm pleased to hear that."

"Ain't against eliminating uncertainty."

They didn't have full info on any other guilds. They had to be the best, the strongest, based on what they *did* know.

"Let's go over our teamwork again. We know Frederica shines against numbers, but Dread, Drag, your pet monsters should give you a lot more options this time around."

"Hell yeah!"

"I do what I can. And if I'm doing it, I wanna win."

"Try and make sure nothing gets through to me, please!"

The Order of the Holy Sword were aiming for victory on their own terms, gathering the pieces required to do so.

The final guild Maple Tree was friendly with was Flame Empire. Their members, too, were talking about the upcoming event and the ninth stratum.

"Everyone's excited, I see."

"Well, yeah. Been ages since we got PvP, and a lot of them are pumped for payback," Shin said, clearly eager himself.

"Nothing wrong with excitement," Misery said.

Marx winced. "Fighting anyone strong just gives me an ulcer…"

"So, what's the plan, Mii? Other than win."

"We will win. But there is much we do not know. The format, the stage, the length of time…we can finalize no plans. We'll hide our cards, and make our choices at the last moment. That will benefit us in the long run."

"That's certainly fair. Anything we do will get noticed, and if they plan against it…that'll hurt."

"Yeah. And Shin, on that point, you've got few weaknesses. I want to take advantage of that."

"I'm in!"

Anyone fighting Mii would reduce fire damage. With Marx, they'd learn to spot traps. For Misery, they'd reduce healing. Each build offered clear countermeasures. Since this game wasn't primarily PvP, there likely weren't many players equipped for all three, but the opposition need merely split up to tackle them.

"And we've got the rest of the guild."

"They're all great…better than me…"

"Hopefully, we can unleash our full might. Misery, Marx, you both make large-scale combat a breeze."

If they had to hold the line, Mii's high-damage spells would turn the tide their way. A power unit who could break through defenses—and that wasn't their only strength.

"What about other guilds? Mii, you're tight with Maple Tree."

"At the moment, I've no plans for specific alliances or rivalries. Naturally, if they're on our side, that would be an advantage, but I'm sure many of us would prefer a rematch."

"Yeah…if they come at us…I'll stop them, this time. Or try. Probably."

"Ha-ha, let the vow stand, man!"

"We'll all work together."

"Not to repeat myself, but an alliance would be welcome, too. I plan to let things play out."

"Cool. Then I'm gonna go train a bit. Be ready to face anybody. Marx, wanna join me? Wanna try some fine control on Splinter Sword."

"Sure…I've got some new traps to try."

"Have fun."

"Will do!"

"Yeah…later…"

Misery waved them off. They'd both gained levels on the eighth stratum, and were ready for the map and the new event.

Once Mii was off with Misery, she softened dramatically.

"Hahhh… PvP?"

"Are you sure you don't want Maple Tree on our side, Mii?"

"Yeah. I meant every word I said! We lost last time, but we're also friends."

"I know. Heh-heh…I wonder which way the wind will blow?"

"Urgh, if they're against us…I'm stressing already."

"Marx and Shin will have your back."

"I'll do what I can. Thanks, Misery."

"No problem."

Each guild thought long and hard about their plans. The stage moved from the eighth to the ninth floor, and the start of the event drew near. When players fought players, no one could predict the victor.

AFTERWORD

Hello to anyone who stumbled across Volume 12 and picked it up. Welcome back—and my deepest thanks—to anyone who's read what came before. I am Yuumikan.

    How time flies. *Bofuri* is already twelve volumes long. Once again, I am reminded that it has only lasted this long thanks to all of you. Lots went down in this volume, and the consequences of that will be seen in the near future. Look forward to it.
    The illustrations show off new gear and items that change how the characters look. I hope you enjoyed seeing that as much as I did. I could not be happier with how much the art enhances the words on the page. As for the TV anime, I want to share news with you as soon as I can. Just as the illustrations bring the characters to life, animation has its own approach to convey the fun of their adventures. I hope you'll all be patient until the time arrives.
    A great many of you are reading the manga, and I know only too well how great everyone involved with that is. I know nothing of manga myself, and approach it like a reader would—marveling at its delights.

AFTERWORD

As if that weren't enough, we've got figures now! This is a whole new endeavor, and I'm beside myself. If you're interested, I hope you'll go for it. Each medium offers a new way to have fun, and I look forward to bringing you more good news in future volumes.

Naturally, I'm doing my level best to ensure the novels are every bit as enjoyable. I hope you'll continue to read *Bofuri* in the future.

Hoping I can bring you more news next time, but for now, let me wrap things up.

Once more, I hope my work matches the efforts of everyone else bringing Maple's adventures to you, so I hope you'll continue reading. And that you're looking forward to Volume 13.

Yuumikan